THE GETAWAY

'The toughest crime novels ever . . . Thompson's fans claim he wrote better books than Hammett did and Chandler. The claim is fatuous; he didn't write their kind of story at all. The first thing to be said about Thompson is that his fiction resembles no one else's. The distinguishing marks of his novels are a high degree of death, a varying degree of comedy, some astonishing play with psychology, and most important – the absence of any moral centre at all. Hammett, Chandler and Macdonald, the so-called hard-boiled writers, were crusading moralists: cynical though their private eyes may be, they restore moral order to their twilight worlds. In Thompson's novels, morality is replaced by ambition. His protagonists are incompetent, usually psychotic, carnivores; like the people they kill, they're losers – they just leave more of a mess before they go'

Peter S. Prescott, *Newsweek*

'Jim Thompson was the king . . . Thompson's vision makes him like nobody else. His is a world peopled with psychopathic killers, expensive sluts, crooked cops, moronic publishers, filthy-minded doctors, cretins, perverts, obsessives . . . Thompson's novels don't have good guys, just anti-heroes and the women who deserve them'

Roderick Thorp

'Jim Thompson had more pistolero savvy than all the so-called *great* American writers . . . Thompson was a hammer to their feather dusters'

Harlan Ellison

'The master of the anti-hero, tough-guy genre'

Publishers Weekly

'Thompson's writing is dense, lucid, idiomatic, musical in its speech rhythms . . . full of weird detours . . . alternatively plaintive and obscene . . . raucous . . . and bitterly funny'

Geoffrey O'Brien, *Village Voice*

James Myers Thompson was born in Oklahoma in 1906. As well as working on an oil pipeline in Texas, as a steeplejack, burlesque actor, professional gambler and seller of bootleg whisky, Thompson wrote for several newspapers, including the *New York Daily News* and *Los Angeles Times Mirror*. During this time he wrote no less than twenty-nine novels, many of which have been made into films in America and France: most notably *The Getaway*, filmed by Sam Peckinpah, starring Steve McQueen; *Pop. 1280*, filmed as *Coup de Torchon*, by Bertrand Tavernier; *The Killer Inside Me*, by Burt Kennedy, starring Stacy Keach; and *A Hell of a Woman*, filmed as *Serie Noire*, by Alain Corneau. He also wrote the screenplays for Stanley Kubrick's *The Killing* and *Paths of Glory*. The last few years of Thompson's life were marred by alcoholism and are chronicled in two works, *The Alcoholics* and *Bad Boy*. When he died at the age of 71, on 7th April 1977, not one of his novels was available in his native America and his reputation had reached its lowest ebb. However, critical opinion of his novels has grown steadily in the intervening years, and Jim Thompson has finally been reinstated amongst the greats like Raymond Chandler, Horace McCoy and Dashiell Hammett.

Also by Jim Thompson

RECOIL
A HELL OF A WOMAN
SAVAGE NIGHT
THE KILL-OFF
WILD TOWN

and published by Corgi Books

THE GETAWAY

Jim Thompson

CORGI BOOKS

THE GETAWAY
A CORGI BOOK 0 552 13350 7

Originally published in Great Britain by Zomba Books

PRINTING HISTORY
Zomba Books edition published 1983
Corgi edition published 1989

Copyright © Estate of Jim Thompson, 1983

This book is set in 11/13pt Mallard
by Busby Typesetting, Exeter.

Corgi Books are published by Transworld Publishers Ltd.,
61-63 Uxbridge Road, Ealing, London W5 5SA, in Australia
by Transworld Publishers (Australia) Pty. Ltd., 15-23 Helles
Avenue, Moorebank, NSW 2170, and in New Zealand by
Transworld Publishers (N.Z.) Ltd., Cnr. Moselle and
Waipareira Avenues, Henderson, Auckland.

Made and printed in Great Britain by
Cox & Wyman Ltd., Reading, Berks

CHAPTER ONE

Carter 'Doc' McCoy had left a morning call for six o'clock, and he was reaching for the telephone the moment the night clerk rang. He had always awakened easily and pleasantly; a man with not a regret for the past, and completely confident and self-assured as he faced each new day. Twelve years of prison routine had merely molded his natural tendencies into habit.

'Why, I slept fine, Charlie,' he said, in his amiably sincere voice. 'Don't suppose I should ask you the same question, eh? Ha-ha! Got my breakfast on the way, have you? Fine, attaboy. You're a gentleman and a scholar, Charlie.'

Doc McCoy hung up the receiver, yawned and stretched agreeably, and sat up in the big, old-fashioned bed. Tipping the shade of the side-street window a little, he glanced at the all-night lunch-room a block away. A Negro busboy was just emerging from the place, a tray covered with a white cloth balanced on one hand. He came up the street at the slow but sullenly steady pace of one who is performing an unavoidable and unfairly imposed task.

5

Doc grinned sympathetically. It was the boy's own fault, of course. He should have known better than to boast to Charlie about the handsome tip 'Mr Kramer' had given him – known that Charlie would relieve him of delivering the tray from then on. Still – Doc went into the bathroom and began to wash – fair was fair; and a boy in a job like that probably needed every nickel he could get.

'You know how it is, Charlie,' he explained ingratiatingly when the clerk arrived with his breakfast. 'Now, with people like you and me, a few bucks either way doesn't make any difference, but – mind giving him this five-spot for me? Tell him I'll drop around and thank him personally when I get back in town.'

The clerk beamed. Him and Mr Kramer! People like *them*! He'd have given the five to that dish jockey even if Mr Kramer hadn't fixed it so that he just about had to.

His face fell suddenly as the full import of Doc's words registered on him. 'W-when you get back? You mean you're leavin'?'

'Just for two-three days, Charlie. A little business matter that can't wait. You bet I'm coming back, and I'm going to tack this time-out onto the end of my vacation.'

'Well—' the clerk was almost weak with relief. 'We-I-I guess you know we're sure glad to have you, Mr Kramer. But believe me, I sure wouldn't be spending no vacation in this place if I was fixed like – if I was you. I'd be cuttin' it up out in Las Vegas, or . . . '

6

'No, no, I don't think you would, Charlie. You're too sensible. You'd get fed up mighty fast, just like I did. So you'd pick out a nice town where you could just laze around and take things easy, and meet some *real* people for a change.' He nodded earnestly, then pressed a bill into the clerk's hand. 'You'll look after everything for me while I'm gone, Charlie? I don't think I'll be taking anything more than a briefcase.'

'You bet! But, gosh, Mr Kramer, you don't need to give me twenty dollars just for . . .'

'But you need it to keep up with those beautiful babes you've got on the string.' Doc urged him genially toward the door. 'Thought I wasn't wise to you, hah? Didn't figure I'd know you were the town lady-killer – ha-ha! Well, take it easy, Charlie.'

Charlie was eager to learn the basis for Mr Kramer's flattering conclusion. But he found that somehow he had gotten out in the hall, and Mr Kramer's door had closed in his face. Dreamily beaming, he went back downstairs to the desk.

Several signals were flashing on the tiny switchboard. Charlie answered them deliberately, stonily unapologetic in the face of inquiries as to whether he'd dropped dead or been on a vacation. Everyone ought to know by this time that he was the only night employee of the Beacon City Hotel. He had the whole shooting match to take care of from nine peeyem until nine ayem, so he had plenty to do besides just stick around the desk. And any time anyone got griped too much about it, they could go to another hotel – the nearest of which was twenty miles away.

Charlie had told a number of gripers where they could head in. Mr Farley, the owner, had told him to. The way Farley – the stingy old jerk! – figured it, hardly anyone stayed at the Beacon City Hotel unless they had to, and he couldn't sell any more rooms with two night employees than he could with one.

Charlie yawned sleepily, and glanced at the oak-cased wall clock. Going behind the key rack, he doused his face at a dingy lavatory and dried on one of the cleaners sections of a soiled roller towel. Lady-killer, he thought, studying his pimpled reflection in the mirror. Oh, you beautiful babes!

Offhand, he could remember seeing only two or three girls in Beacon City who might even remotely qualify as truly beautiful babes; and none of these, as the saying is, had been able to see him at all. But – well, maybe he just hadn't been lookin' sharp enough. He hadn't gone about things right. Because that Mr Kramer was one might-ee shrewd *hombre*, and if he had a fella sized up in a certain way . . .!

Leaving the desk, Charlie took up a position before the lobby window; hands folded behind him, rocking back and forth on the balls of his feet. The glass was so dusty and fly-specked as to serve inadequately as a mirror, and in it he was only mildly unappetizing.

Rose Hip, the Chinese laundryman's lovely daughter, tripped by on her way to business

8

college. Charlie winked at her, and she stuck out her tongue at him. Charlie smirked knowingly.

There just wasn't much of anything stirring after that. As Charlie put it, you could have fired a machine gun down Main Street without hitting a soul. It was due to the recent change-over to daylight saving time, Charlie thought; folks hadn't got used to it yet. Maybe the clock said it was getting kind of late – seventeen minutes of eight – but it still wasn't seven to the people.

Charlie started to turn away from the window; then, hesitantly, hearing a familiar creak of cartwheels, he faced it again. The woman was old 'Crazy' Cvec, the town scavenger. Her wobbly cart was piled high with cardboard cartons, rags and bottles. She was dressed in a ragged mother hubbard, an ancient picture hat, and toeless tennis shoes. A frayed cigar butt protruded from the corner of her sunken-in mouth.

When Charlie winked at her, her gums parted in an insane cackle and the butt dropped down the front of her gown. This sent her into a paroxysm of crazy cackling, which she concluded by gripping the handle of the cart and kicking friskily backward with both feet. Charlie giggled lewdly. Lifting a foot, he shook his leg in the manner of a man who has got a bee up his trousers. Then . . .

'Well, I'll be damned,' said a jeering voice. 'Yes, sir, I will be damned.'

It was Mack Wingate, bank guard and long-time

resident of the hotel. Mack Wingate, dressed in his crisp gray-blue uniform and cap; his plump face twisted in a look of acid astonishment.

'So that's your girl friend,' he said. 'You and Crazy Cvec. Well, I guess you're gettin' the best of the bargain at that.'

'Now, l-listen you!' The clerk was scarlet-faced, tremulously furious. 'You better not – go and fill your inkwells! Clean out the spittoons!'

' 'Spect you're feeling pretty proud, hey, Charlie? Me, now, I like 'em kind of ma-chure myself, and you sure got to admit old Crazy's matured. Hard to tell which stinks the ripest, her or the . . .'

'Yah!' said Charlie desperately. 'I guess you know, don't you? You know all about her, don't you, Mack?'

'Now, don't you worry, boy. I know a real love match when I see it, and I ain't gonna come between you.'

'Dang you, Mack! You –' he searched wildly for some effective threat. 'You – I'm warning you for the last time, Mack! No more cooking in your room. You do it just once more, and . . .'

Wingate belched, emanating an odor of day-old rolls and coffee. 'But you goin' to let me bake your weddin' cake, ain't you, Charlie? Or was you fig-urin' on Crazy pickin' one up from the garbage?'

Charlie made a strangled sound. His shoulders slumped helplessly. He just wasn't any match for the bank guard. No one in town was. Anything you said to him, why, he just ignored it, and kept coming at you harder than ever. And he never got

10

off of you until he got someone better to ride – which would be a darned long time in this case.

The guard gripped one of his inert hands, and shook it warmly. 'Want to be the first to congratulate you, Charlie. You're really gettin' something when you get Crazy. Wouldn't say what it was exactly, but . . .'

'G-get out of here,' Charlie whispered. 'Y-you tell anyone about this, an' I'll . . .'

'Sure, now. Sure, you're kind of up in the air,' said Mack Wingate with hideous sympathy. 'It ain't every day in the week that a man gets hisself engaged. So don't you worry about sendin' out no announcements. I'll see to it that everyone . . .'

Charlie turned abruptly and went behind the desk. Mack laughed, snorted wonderingly and started across the street.

On the opposite side, he stood poised for a moment, hand on the butt of his gun, and looked deliberately from left to right. Some two blocks away a car was slowly rounding the corner. No one was immediately nearby, except a storekeeper sweeping off his walk and a farmer driving a spring-seat wagon – and both were well known to him. Mack turned and unlocked the bank door.

Reaching quickly inside, he shut off the automatic alarm. He stepped up to and across the threshold; and then – as it appeared to Charlie at least – Mack tripped over his own feet and went sprawling into the darkened interior.

The clerk hugged himself delightedly. He wanted to see the expression on Mack's face when he stuck his head out the door for a quick look around before locking it again. After a stupid tumble like that, he'd be a cinch to look out, Charlie figured. He'd be scared to death that someone'd seen him and would say something about it – a bank guard that couldn't do any better than that! And you could just bet that someone was going to, if Mack said anything about something else.

Unfortunately, Charlie couldn't go on watching the door. Because just then, Mr Kramer's light flashed on the switchboard. And he was one person Charlie never kept waiting.

And 'Mr Kramer', that prince of men, would be the first to say so.

CHAPTER TWO

It was doubtful whether Rudy Torrento had ever enjoyed a good night's sleep in his life. He was afraid of the dark. Early in his infancy, the night and the sleep that was normal to it had become indelibly associated with terror; with being stumbled over, smothered under a drunken mountain of flesh. With being yanked up by the hair, held helpless by one meaty hand while the other beat him into insensibility.

He was afraid to sleep, and equally fearful of awaking; from the dawn of his memory, the days had also been identified with terror. In the latter case, however, his fear was of a different kind. A cornered rat might feel as Rudy Torrento felt on coming into full consciousness. Or a snake with its head caught beneath a forked stick. It was an insanely aggressive, outrageously furious fear; a self-frightening, self-poisoning emotion, gnawing acidly at the man whose existence depended upon it.

He was paranoid; incredibly sharp of instinct; filled with animal cunning. He was also very vain. On the one hand, then, he was confident that Doc McCoy intended to kill him, as soon as he served Doc's purposes, and on the other, he could not admit it. Doc was too smart to tangle with Rudy Torrento; he'd know that no one pulled a cross on Rudy.

When the first gray streaks of daylight seeped through the boarded-up windows of the old farmhouse, Rudy sat up groaning, eyes still closed, and began a frantic pummeling and massaging of his ribs. They had all been broken and rebroken before he was old enough to run. By now, they had long since grown together in a twisted mass of cartilage, bone and scar tissue, which ached horribly when he became chilled or when he lay long in one position.

Having pounded and rubbed them into a degree of comfort, he fumbled among his blankets until he found whiskey, cigarettes and matches. He took a long drink of the liquor, lighted and inhaled deeply on a cigarette, and suddenly – with planned suddenness – opened his eyes.

The punk, Jackson, was staring at him. Being a little slow on the trigger, compared with Rudy at least, he continued to stare for a moment longer.

Torrento beamed at him with sinister joviality. 'Got a mug like a piece of pie, ain't I, kid? A chunk with the big end down.'

'Huh – what?' The kid suddenly came alive. 'Uh – ain't that funny? Guess I must've been sittin' here asleep with my eyes wide open.'

Rudy's lips parted in a wolfish, humorless grin.

14

He said yes, sir, it was funny as all hell. But not nearly so funny, of course, as the way he himself looked. 'My maw's doctor did that for me, Jackie boy. The one that took care of her when I was born. I had a pretty big noggin on me, y'see, so just to make things nice and easy for her he kinda sloped it off to a point. That's how I got the handle – "Piehead" Torrento. Didn't know I had a real first name for a long time. Maybe you'd like to call me Piehead too, huh, Jackie boy?'

The kid jerked his head nervously. Even in the two-bit underworld of window smashers and jack-rollers which had been his recruited ground, Rudy's sensitivity about his appearance was a legend. You didn't call him Piehead any more than you'd've called Benny Siegel 'Buggsy.' The mere mention of pie in his presence was apt to inspire him to murderous fury.

'You need some coffee, Rudy,' the kid said mannishly. 'Some good hot coffee and a couple of them snazzy sandwiches I bought last night.'

'I asked you a question!'

'That's right, that's right, all right,' the kid murmured vaguely, and he poured a steaming cup of coffee from the vacuum bottle; diffidently extended it, with a sandwich, toward the gangster.

For a moment Rudy remained motionless, staring at him out of fixed, too-bright eyes. Then, abruptly, he burst into laughter, for he had remembered something very funny. The kind of thing that would amuse him when nothing else would.

'You got a lot of guts, Jackson,' he said, snorting and choking over the words. 'A real gutsy ginzo, that's you.'

'Well,' the punk, said modestly, 'I wouldn't want to say so myself, but most anyone that knows me will tell you that when it comes to a showdown, why, uh . . .'

'Uh-huh. Well, we'll see, Jackson. We'll see what you got inside of you.' Again Rudy was convulsed. And then, with one of his mercurial changes of mood, he was overwhelmed with pity for the kid.

'Eat up, Jackie,' he said. 'Catch onto some of that coffee and chow yourself.'

They ate. Over second cups of coffee, Rudy passed cigarettes and held a light for the boy. Jackson felt encouraged to ask questions, and for once the gangster did not reply with insults or order him to shut up.

'Well, Doc didn't just *happen* to pick this Beacon City job,' he said. 'Doc never just happens to do anything. He has this plan, see, so he goes looking for exactly the right place to fit into it. Probably scouted around for two-three months, traveled over half a dozen counties, before he settled on Beacon City. First, he looks for a bank that ain't a member of the Federal Reserve System. Then – huh?' Rudy frowned at the interruption. 'Well, why the hell do you think, anyway?'

'Oh. Oh, I see,' the kid said quickly. 'The Feds don't come in on the case, right, Rudy?'

'Right. The talk is that they're fixin' to cut

16

themselves in on any bank robbery, but they ain't got around to it yet. Well, so anyway he checks that angle, and then he checks on interest rates. If a bank's paying little or nothing on savings, y'see, it means they got a lot more dough than they can loan out. So that tips Doc off on the most likely prospects, and all he has to do then is check their statements of condition – you've seen them printed in the newspapers, haven't you? How much dough they've got on hand and so on?'

'I've seen 'em, but they never made any sense to me. I mean, well, it always looks to me like they got just enough to pay their bills with. They ain't got any more at the end of the year than they had in the beginning.'

Rudy chuckled. 'I'm with you, Jackie. But they mean plenty to Doc. He can read them things like they were funny books.'

'Plenty foxy, huh? A real brain.' The kid shook his head admiringly, not noticing Rudy's sudden scowl. 'But how come we're goin' so far out of our way to skim out, Rudy? Why go all the way up and across the country when we're only a few hundred miles from the border here?'

'You don't like it?' said Rudy. 'You stupid sap, they'd be expecting us to travel in a beeline.'

'Sure, sure,' Jackson mumbled hastily. 'What about that place we're holing up in? They really can't extradite us from there? Not no way?'

'You got nothing to worry about,' Rudy told him. And again, for the moment, he was pitying. 'There's this one old geezer, El Rey – that

17

means The King, y'know, in Mex – well, him and his family, his sons and grandsons and nephews and so on, they run the place. The state or province or what the hell ever it's called. They really run it, know what I mean? They're the cops and the judges and the prosecutors and everything else. So long as you pay off and don't make no trouble with the locals, you're settin' pretty.'

The kid whistled appreciatively. 'But, look. What's to keep 'em from grabbing a guy's loot, and knocking him off? I mean – uh – well, I guess that wouldn't be so smart, would it? The word would get around, and they wouldn't get no more customers.'

'Just about one like you, and they wouldn't want any more,' Rudy grunted. 'You'd spread them idiot germs around, an' the whole population would turn stupid.'

'I'm sorry – I didn't mean nothin'.'

'And you don't. A big fat zero, that's you,' Rudy said. And that was the end of his pity.

They had shaved late the night before, and they managed a wash by tipping the water jug over one another's hands. They combed their hair, brushed their clothes thoroughly with a whisk broom, and then, completely dressed, checked each other's appearance.

They wore dark suits, white shirts, and hats of a semi-Homburg type. Except for their shoulder-holstered guns and their briefcases, they took nothing with them when they went out the back

18

door to their car. The briefcases were large – much larger than they looked – and bore a bold-lettered OFFICE OF STATE above an equally bold-stamped BANK EXAMINER. The car, with its immensely souped-up motor, appeared to be just another black, low-priced sedan.

Jackson climbed in with the briefcase, swung open the door on the driver's side and started the motor. Rudy peered around the corner of the abandoned house. A truck had just passed on the way into Beacon City. There was nothing else in sight. Rudy leaped into the car, gunned the motor and sent it rocketing down the weed-bordered lane to the highway.

He whipped it into the highway, wheels skidding. He relaxed, slowing its speed, taking a long, deep breath. Maybe it wouldn't have mattered if someone had seen them coming out of the lane. They could have turned into it accidentally, or maybe to fix a tire on the buggy. Still, that was maybe, and maybes were bad stuff. A very small one, one that hadn't seemed big enough to kick out of the way, had tumbled Rudy the Piehead into Alcatraz for a ten-year fall.

He kept one eye on his wristwatch as he drove. They entered town on schedule to the minute, and Rudy spoke to the kid in a tight, quiet voice. 'Now, this is going to be all right,' he said. 'Doc knows his job, I know mine. You're green, but it don't make any difference. All you got to do is just what you're told – just follow my lead – and we'll roll through it like smoke through a chimney.'

19

'I – I'm not afraid, Rudy.'

'Be afraid. What the hell? Just keep the cork on it.'

At the corner two blocks above the bank, Rudy slowed the car to a crawl, swinging a little wide so that he could see down the main street. They were on schedule, but Mack Wingate, the bank guard, wasn't. Automatically, Rudy killed the motor, then began to fumble futilely with the starter. The kid turned to him, white-faced.

'R-Rudy – w-what's the . . .'

'Easy. Easy, Jackie boy,' Rudy said, the words quiet, his nerves screaming murder. 'Guard's a little late, see, but it don't mean a thing. If he doesn't show fast, we'll circle again and . . .'

The guard came out of the hotel then, started briskly across the street. Rudy stalled a few seconds longer, and then smoothly started the motor and rounded the corner. In little more than a minute after the guard had entered the bank, Rudy was parking in front of it.

He and Jackson got out of the car on opposite sides, the boy lingering a step or so behind him. Crossing the walk, their briefcases turned to display the official stamp on them, Rudy gave a curtly pleasant nod to the storekeeper and received a vacant stare in return. Leaning on his broom, the man continued to stare as Rudy rapped on the bank door.

The kid was panting heavily, crowding on Rudy's heels. The gangster called, 'Hey, Wingate! Hurry it up,' and then turned a flat, steady gaze on the storekeeper. 'Yes?' he said. 'Something wrong, mister?'

'Just about to ask you the same,' the man said pertly. 'Bank ain't in no trouble, is she?'

Very slowly, his eyes hardening, Rudy looked him over from head to foot. 'The bank's not in any trouble,' he said. 'You trying to make some for it?'

'Me?' the man's head waggled in anxious protest. 'I was just makin' talk, you know. Just joking.'

'There's a law against that kind of joke,' Rudy told him. 'Maybe you'd better get a new one, huh?'

The storekeeper nodded feebly. He turned and tottered into his establishment, and Rudy and the kid entered the bank.

Rudy snatched up the key from the floor, and relocked the door. The kid let out a croak of amazement, one finger pointing shakily to the guard's sprawled body. 'Lookit! It l-looks like he'd had a p-pencil pushed through his head.'

'What are you, the coroner?' Rudy blazed. 'Get his cap on! Peel out of your jacket, and put on his!'

'That fellow outside, Rudy. D-do you suppose he'll . . .'

Torrento gave him a stinging backhanded slap. Then, as the kid reeled, he caught his lapels and yanked him up to within an inch of his face. 'There's just two people you got to worry about, know what I mean? Just you and me. And you keep on playin' the jerk, there'll only be one of

21

us.' Rudy gave him a hard bearing-down shake. 'You got that? Think you can remember it?'

The glaze drained out of Jackson's eyes. He nodded; spoke quite calmly. 'I'm all right now, Rudy. You'll see.'

He put on the guard's jacket and cap, pulling the bill low over his forehead. Then, since Rudy was afraid that the dead man might panic the other employees into hysteria, they pitched his body into the railed-off desk area and pulled a rug over it.

Back in the lobby proper again, Rudy put the kid through a final rehearsal. He wasn't supposed to peek out the door, of course. Make like he was, by rattling the shade a little, but not really do it. And when he opened the door, he wasn't to show nothing of himself but his jacket sleeve and maybe the bill of his cap.

'You don't need to sell 'em, see? They don't know anything's wrong, or if they do there's nothing we can do about it. Now –' Rudy tapped on the glass top of one of the high, marble-pedestaled customer's desks. 'Now, here's the code again. Here's how you'll know it's one of the wage slaves and not some Johnny-ahead-of-time wanting change for a quarter. There'll be a *knock-knock-knock*, like that, see? Then a *knock and another knock*. Three and two.'

'I get it,' Jackson nodded. 'I remember, Rudy.'

'Some code, huh? Must have took Doc two or three minutes to figure out with a pair of binoculars. But just the three employees will use

22

the code; they'll show between now and eight-thirty. The big cheese gets here about a quarter of, and he don't knock. Just rattles the door latch and says, "Wingate, Wingate!" '

Rudy glanced at the clock, gestured. They took up positions on opposite sides of the door, Rudy drew his gun, and there was a knock-knock-knock, and a knock – knock.

The kid hesitated, freezing for a split second. Then as Rudy nodded to him, gravely encouraging, his nerve returned and he opened the door.

CHAPTER THREE

Four months before, when it was certain that Doc
was getting a pardon on his second and last jolt,
his wife, Carol, had quarreled violently with him
while visiting the prison. She announced that
she was suing him for divorce, and had actually
started proceedings against him; leaving them in
abeyance, ostensibly, until she could acquire
the money to carry them through. Soon afterward, with the announced intention of changing
her name and making a new start in life, she
boarded a train for New York – coach-class,
unreserved seat – and that seemed to be that.

Except that she did not go to New York, did
not and had never meant to get a divorce, and
had in fact never for a moment entertained the
slightest desire for any life other than the one
she had.

Back in the beginning, perhaps, she had had
some conscience-impelled notion of reforming
Doc. But she could not think of that now without a downward quirk of her small mouth, a
wince born more of bewilderment than em-

barrassment at the preposterousness of her one-time viewpoint.

Reform? Change? Why, and to what? The terms were meaningless. Doc had opened a door for her, and she had entered into, adopted and been adopted by, a new world. And it was difficult to believe now that any other had ever existed. Doc's amoral outlook had become hers. In a sense, she had become more like Doc than Doc himself. More engagingly persuasive when she chose to be. Harder when hardness seemed necessary.

Doc had teased her about this a time or two until he saw that it annoyed her. 'A little more of *that*,' he would say, 'and we'll send you back to the bookstacks.' And while Carol wasn't angered by his funning – it was almost impossible to be angry with Doc – neither did she appreciate it. It gave her a vague feeling of indecency, of being unfairly exposed. She had felt much the same way when her parents per-sisted in exhibiting one of her baby pictures; a trite display of infant nudity sprawled on a woolly white rug.

It was her picture, all right, and yet it really wasn't her. So why not forget it? Forget also that more than two decades after the picture was taken, she was just about as dishwater-dull, dumb and generally undesirable as a young woman could be.

She had been working as a librarian then; living with her stodgy, middle-aged parents and daily settling deeper into the pattern of spinsterhood. She had no life but the lifeless one of her job and home. She was fine-featured, her small body beautifully full. But people saw only the dowdy 'sensible' clothes and the primness of her manner, and thought of her as plain and even homely.

Then Doc had come along – still on parole, he was already doing research on another job, and he had instantly seen the woman that she really was; and with his easy smile, his amiable persuasiveness, his inoffensive persistence, he had pulled that woman right out of her shell. Oh, it hadn't been a matter of minutes, of course. Or even days. She had been pretty skittish, as a matter of fact. Snubbing and glaring at him; putting him in what she thought of as 'his place'. But somehow you just couldn't do things like that with Doc. Somehow they seemed to hurt you worse than they did him. So she had relented – just a little – and the next minute, seemingly, she was through that marvelous door. And kicking it firmly shut behind her.

Her parents had washed their hands of her. *Some parents!* she thought contemptuously. She had lost her friends, her position in the community. *Some friends, some position!* She had acquired a police record.

Carol (Ainslee) McCoy. No alias. Photo and f-prints reclaimed by court order. Three arrests; no trials or convictions. Susp. of complicity murder, armed robbery, bank robbery, in consort with husb. 'Doc' (Carter) McCoy. May work as steno; general office. May appear attractive or unattractive, very friendly or unfriendly. Five feet, two in.; 110lbs.; gray to green eyes; brown, black, red or light blonde hair. Age 30-35. Approach with caution.

Carol smiled to herself, winked at her reflection in the car's rearview mirror. *Some record!* It had more holes in it than their little fat heads.

Since her ostensible departure for New York, she had been working as a restaurant night cashier in a city some five hundred miles away. Under a different name, of course, and looking not at all like she looked now. Yesterday morning she had quit the job (to join her Army-sergeant husband in Georgia), slept all day, taken delivery on a new car and started driving toward Beacon City.

At eight o'clock in the morning she was within sixty miles of the town. After breakfasting on the rolls and coffee she had brought with her, and a quick wash in a filling station, she felt quite rested and high-spirited despite the long hours at the wheel.

Her rollneck cashmere sweater snugly emphasized her narrowness of waist, the flaring fullness below it and the rich contours above. A long-billed airman's cap was cocked pertly on her head, and her hair – tawny brown now – flounced out from beneath it in a jaunty ponytail. Her bobby-socked ankles tapered up into a pair of slacks which were really much less than skin-tight, although they did seem pretty well filled to capacity in at least one area.

She looked heartbreakingly young and gay. She looked – well, what was wrong with the word – sexy? Tingling pleasantly, Carol decided there was nothing at all wrong with it.

She had not seen Doc since their phony quarrel at the prison. Their only contact had been through brief, cautious and emotionally un-satisfying long-distance phone calls. That was the way it had to be, and Carol, like Doc – being so much a part of Doc – did not quarrel with what had to be. Still, that did not keep her from being almost deliriously happy that the long months of their separation were over.

Doc would be very pleased with her, she knew. With the way she looked; with everything she had done.

The car was a flashy yellow convertible. Stacked along with the baggage on the rear seat and floor were golf clubs, fishing rods, tennis rackets and other vacation impedimenta. The bags were bright with the stickers of assorted hotels and tourist courts. One of them contained a cap similar to her own, sunglasses and a gaudy sports jacket. That was all it held since it was meant to accommodate the loot from the bank.

They would be very conspicuous as they traveled, and the conspicuousness would give them safety. The more obvious and out in the open a thing was, Doc had taught her, the less likely it was to attract attention.

She began to drive slower, to glance more and more frequently at the dashboard clock and the speedometer's mileage indicator. At nine she saw a puff of black smoke spout up in the distance; then a billowing oily cloud of it. Carol nodded approvingly.

Doc was right on schedule, as always. The smoke signaled the successful accomplishment of the second half of his part in the robbery. Which meant, since one part was dependent upon the other, that he had also pulled off the first one.

She took another look at the clock, drove still more slowly. At the crest of a hill she stopped the car and began raising the canvas top. A truck and two cars went past, the driver of one slowing as though to offer help. Carol waved him on in a way that let him know that she meant it, then slid back behind the wheel.

She lighted a cigarette, flipped it away after a puff or two, and stared narrowly through the windshield. Nine-fifteen – no, it was almost nine-twenty. And she hadn't got the signal yet, the winking left headlight. True, one of those distant oncoming cars had suddenly disappeared from the highway – there went another one right now – but that didn't mean anything. There were many turnoffs; up through tree-lined farm lanes, or cutting between one farm and another.

In any event, Doc never made any last-minute

changes in plans. If changes seemed indicated, he simply dropped the job, either permanently or until a later date. So, since he had said there would be a signal . . .

Carol started the car. She took a gun out of the glove compartment, shoved it into the waistband of her slacks and pulled her sweater over it. Then she drove on – *fast!*

Doc McCoy's breakfast had cooled before he could get rid of Charlie, the night clerk. But he ate it with an enjoyment which may or may not have been as real as was apparent. It was hard to tell with Doc: to know whether he actually did like something or someone as well as he seemed to. Nor is it likely that Doc himself knew. Agreeability was his stock in trade. He had soaked up so much of it that everything he touched seemed roseately transformed.

Doc's beaming good nature and the compelling personality that was its outgrowth were largely owing to his father, the widowed sheriff of a small down-south county. To compensate for the loss of his wife, the elder McCoy kept his house filled with company. Liking his job – and knowing that he would never get another half as good – he made sure of keeping it. He had never been known to say no, even to a mob's request for a prisoner. He was ready at all times to fiddle for a wedding or weep at a wake. No poker session, cockfight or stag party was considered complete without his presence; yet he was a steadfast church communicant and the ever-present guest at the most genteel social gatherings. Inevitably, he came to be the best-liked man in the county, the one man who everyone honestly regarded as a friend. He also was the grossest incompetent and the most costly ornament in the county's body politic. But the only person who had ever faulted him – an opposition candidate – had barely escaped a wrathful lynching party.

Doc, then, was born popular; into a world where he was instantly liked and constantly reassured of his welcome. Everyone smiled, everyone was friendly, everyone was anxious to please him. Without being spoiled – his father's strictly male household took care of that – he acquired an unshakable belief in his own merit; a conviction that he not only would be but should be liked wherever he went. And holding such a conviction, he inevitably acquired the pleasant traits and personality to justify it.

Rudy Torrento planned to kill Doc, but he was resentfully drawn to him.

Doc intended to kill Rudy, but he by no means disliked Torrento. He only liked him less than he did certain other people.

His breakfast finished, Doc stacked the dishes neatly on the tray and set it outside his door. The maid was vacuuming the hall and Doc told her of his impending departure ('for a few days') and that she need not bother with his room until he had left. He inquired into the health of her rheumatic husband, complimented her on her new shoes, gave her a five-dollar tip, and smilingly closed the door.

He bathed, shaved and began to dress.

He was five feet, ten and one-half inches tall, and he weighed roughly one hundred and seventy-pounds. His face was a little long, his mouth wide and a trifle thin-lipped, his eyes gray and wideset. His graying, sand-colored hair was very thin on top. In one of his sloping, unostentatiously powerful shoulders were two bullet scars. Aside from that, there was nothing to distinguish him from any number of forty-year-old men.

The stock and barrel of a rifle were slung by loops inside his topcoat. Doc took them out, hung the coat back in the closet, and began to assemble them. The stock was from an ordinary twenty-two rifle. The barrel, as well as the rest of the gun proper, had either been made or made over by Doc. Its most distinctive feature was a welded-on cylinder, fitted at one end with a plunger. It looked like, and was, a small air pump.

Doc slid a twenty-two slug into the breech, closed and locked it and rocked the slug into place. He began to pump, pumping harder as the resistance inside the air chamber grew. When he could no longer depress the plunger, he gave it several quick turns, sealing the end of the cylinder.

He smoked a cigarette and scanned the morning newspaper which Charlie had brought with his breakfast, pausing now and then to pick idly at an incipient hangnail. He reweighed his decision to dispose of Rudy, and could see no reason to change it. No reason, at least, of sufficient importance.

When they reached the West Coast, they would need to hole up temporarily; to reconsider, switch cars and break trail generally, before jumping into Mexico. It was wise to do that at any rate, even though it might not be absolutely necessary. And Rudy had lined up a place where they could take temporary sanctuary. It was a small tourist court, owned by some distant relatives of his. They were naturalized citizens, an almost painfully honest, elderly couple. But they had an unreasoning fear of the police, brought with them from the old country, and they were even more terrified of Rudy. So, reluctantly, they had submitted to his demands, on this occasion and several others.

Doc was confident that he could handle them quite well without Rudy. He was confident that they would be even more rather than less cooperative if they knew that he had disposed of their fearsome kinsman.

Glancing at his watch, Doc lighted another cigarette and picked up the rifle. Standing back in the concealing shadows of the room, he took aim through the window, one eye squinted against the smoke from the dangling cigarette. The bank guard was due any minute now. He . . .

There was a knock on the door. Doc hesitated

for a split second, then crossed the room in two long strides and opened the door a few inches. The maid thrust a handful of towels at him.

'Sorry to bother you, Mr Kramer. Thought you might be needin' these.'

'Why, that's very thoughtful of you,' Doc said. 'Just a moment and I'll . . .'

'Now, that's all right, Mr Kramer. You given me too much already.'

'But I insist,' Doc said pleasantly. 'You wait right here, Rosie.'

Leaving the door ajar, he wheeled back across the room and raised the rifle, sighting it as he moved. Mack Wingate was just stepping across the bank's threshold, had almost disappeared into its dark interior. Doc triggered the gun and there was a sharp, sighing sound, like the sudden emission of breath.

He didn't wait to see the guard fall; when Doc shot at something he hit it. With a more powerful rifle his aim would have been just as accurate at five hundred yards as it had been at fifty.

He gave the maid a dollar bill, again thanking her for her courtesy. Closing and relocking the door, he got the clerk on the phone.

'Charlie, does that train into the city leave at nine-twenty or nine-thirty? Fine, that's what I thought. No, no cab, thanks. I can use a little walk.'

He hung up the phone, reloaded the rifle, and again pumped up the pressure. He unfastened the stock, locked it up in his briefcase, and put the

34

rest back in the loops of the topcoat.

He lifted the coat out, draped it loosely over one arm. He walked back and forth with it for a moment, then nodded with satisfaction and hung it back in the closet. Rudy wouldn't expect him to have the rifle. It should come as a complete surprise to him. But just in case it didn't . . .

I'll think of something, Doc assured himself. And went to work on a more immediate problem.

His luggage contained an unusual number of toiletries: bath salts, hair tonics and the like. More accurately, it contained the *containers* of these items, which were filled not with what their labels indicated but such oddly assorted things as naphtha, crude oil, a gauze-wrapped quarter-stick of dynamite, and the movements from two watches.

They formed the ingredients of two incendiary smoke bombs. Doc began to assemble them, first spreading the newspaper out on the bed to protect its coverings. A few fine beads of sweat formed on his forehead. The movements of his fingers were sure, but extremely delicate.

The dynamite itself – which he sliced into two pieces – he regarded as safe, and a mere quarter-stick of it as virtually harmless (to one familiar with its action) even if exploded. No, dynamite was all right. Dinah was easygoing, tolerating almost anything short of outrage. The danger lay in that cute little black cap she wore when being readied for action. They – the percussion caps – were about the size of an after-dinner mint,

35

and their behavior was anything but good. And tiny as they were, one of them was more than enough to remove a man's hand.

Doc was glad when his job was finished, glad that he would never again have to take on a similar job. The bombs could have been purchased ready-made, of course, but Doc distrusted the purveyors of such items. They might talk; besides, they lacked the incentive to turn out top-grade merchandise, anything less than which was apt to prove fatal to the purchaser.

Doc put the bombs in his wastebasket and crumpled the soiled newspaper over them. He scrubbed his hands in the bathroom and turned down the turned-up cuffs of his shirt. For no conscious reason, he sighed.

He'd been on tougher jobs than this one, but never one where so much depended on its success. Everything he had was on the line here; everything that he and Carol had. He was pushing forty-one. She was almost fourteen years younger. So, one more fall, one more prison stretch and – and that would be that.

The thoughts stirred muddily in the bottom of his mind. Unrecognized and unadmitted; manifested only in an unconscious sigh.

He had not taken another look at the bank, since seeing that Rudy and the kid had gotten in all right. He'd had work to do, and there'd been no point in looking. If there was trouble, he'd be able to hear it.

Now, however, he looked again, and was just in time to see the bank president enter its door.

The door closed abruptly, almost catching the heel of his shoe. Doc winced and shook his head, unconsciously as he had sighed.

It was ten minutes of nine. Doc adjusted his tie and put on his suit jacket. Now it was five minutes of. He picked up the wastebasket and stepped out into the hall.

He went down the faded red carpet to the end of the hall, then turned right into a short side corridor. A metal trash can stood between the back stairs and the side-street window. Doc poked the papers into the can, idly glancing up and down the street.

His luck was far better than he could have hoped for.

A flatbed farm truck was parked rear end first at the curb. Next to it was a sedan, its windows rolled up tightly. But next to them, parked to windward of them, was another truck – loaded almost to the level of the hotel's second-floor windows.

And what it was loaded with was baled hay!

Doc gave the street another quick up and down glance. Then he tossed the bombs, lofting one between the truck's cab and bed, the other onto the load of hay.

He picked up the wastebasket and returned to his room. It was two minutes of nine now – two minutes before the bombs were set to explode – and three or four people were gathered in front of the bank, waiting for it to open.

Doc completed his arrangements for leaving, slowly counting off the seconds.

CHAPTER FOUR

The time lock on the bank's vault was set for eight-fifty. Slightly more than ten minutes later, Rudy and Jackson had cleared it of cash – dollar bills and coins excepted – and several thick packages of negotiable securities.

The banker lay sprawled on the floor, half-dead from Rudy's pistol-whipping. Stumbling over his unconscious body, Rudy gave him a savage kick in the face, turned half-crazed eyes upon the kid. The fear had filled him now, the furious outraged fear of a cornered rat. It would simmer down in time, solidify into the murderous trigger-quick wiliness which had guided him in and out of so many tight places. Which forced him to survive long after the withered inner man had cried out for the peace of death. Now, however, there was nothing but the raging fear, and he had to strike out at something. At anything.

'You hear anything out there?' He jerked his head toward the street. 'Well, did you?'

'Hear anything? W-what . . .'

'The bombs, you long-eared jerk! Any commotion.'

'Huh-uh. But I don't guess we could, could we, Rudy? I mean, there in the vault we – N-no! D-don't!'

The kid strangled on a scream. He tried to claw the gun from his belt. Then he toppled forward, clutching at his half-disemboweled abdomen; at the guts which Torrento had mockingly credited him with having.

Rudy giggled. He made a sound that was strangely akin to a sob. Then he wiped his knife on a blotter, returned it to his pocket and picked up the two briefcases.

He carried them to the bank door, set them down again. He turned and looked meditatively at the bank's three employees. They were scattered about the lobby floor, their mouths sealed with tape, their wrists and ankles bound with more tape. They looked at him, their eyes rolling to show the whites, and Rudy hesitantly fingered his knife.

They'd have him tabbed for the robbery, for killing the kid. And if things broke wrong, Doc would doubtless manage to tag him with the guard's death. Trust Doc to keep himself in the clear, him and his smart little sneak of a wife! But anyway, these yokels could finger him – pick his wedge-shaped map out of a million mug shots. So as long as he couldn't be fried or have his neck popped but once anyhow, why not . . .

He took the knife out again. He went from employee to employee, slashing the bond of their ankles, kicking and cursing and yanking them to their feet.

Shoving them ahead of him, he herded them back inside the vault. He swung the door shut on them, gave the knob a few spins.

There'd been no point in killing them. He'd been seen coming into the joint, and he was a cinch to be seen leaving. There was a hell of a racket outside and it was growing by the second, and even in here you could get a whiff of smoke. But still, someone, a lot of someones, would see him leave. The best he could hope for was that none of 'em would try to do anything about it.

None of 'em did. Doc had figured right. They had too much else to be interested in to pay any attention to him. And after all, what was so funny about a guy coming out of a bank during banking hours?

The side street was jammed with people, surging back towards the walks occasionally when the wind-driven smoke threatened to envelop them. Sparks showered upward from the burning hay. A gas tank exploded, sending a speckled fountain of fire into the air. The crowd roared, jamming back into the intersection, and the people in the intersection tried to push forward. Several men in red helmets were scurrying about, shouting and gesturing futilely. Other red-helmeted men were lunging up the street, dragging a two-wheel hose car behind them. The bell in the courthouse cupola tolled steadily.

Rudy loaded the briefcases into the car. He

40

made a U-turn, honking for a couple of yokels to get out of the way, and headed out of town.

A block away, Doc stepped down from the walk to the street and climbed in with him. They rode on, Rudy grinning meanly to himself as he noted the careless caution with which Doc handled his coat. McCoy asked him how they had made out.

'Two hundred in bonds. Maybe a hundred and forty in cash.'

'A hundred and forty?' Doc's eyes flicked at him. 'I see. Must've been a lot of ones and silver.'

'So maybe there's more, dammit! You think I figured it up on an addin' machine?'

'Now, Rudy,' Doc said soothingly, 'no offense. How did it go with the youngster?'

'What d'you mean, how'd it go? How'd you plan it to go?'

'Of course. Too bad,' Doc said vaguely. 'I always feel bad when something like that is necessary.'

Rudy snorted. He jammed a cigarette into his mouth, put his left hand in his jacket pocket, ostensibly seeking a match. It came out with a heavy automatic which he leveled across his lap.

'Get rid of the rifle, Doc. Toss it out in the ditch.'

'Might as well.' Doc didn't appear to notice the automatic. 'Doesn't look like we're going to need it.'

He lifted the rifle, muzzle first, and dropped it out the window. Rudy let out another snort.

'Doesn't look like we're gonna need it!' he mocked. 'Well, you ain't going to need that rod in your jacket either, Doc, so – *don't move for it!* Just take the jacket off and toss it in the back seat.'

'Listen, Rudy . . .'

'Do it!'

Doc did it. Rudy made him lean forward, then backward, swiftly scanning his trousers. He nodded, gave Doc permission to light a cigarette. Doc turned a little in the seat, eyes sorrowful beneath the brim of his hat.

'This doesn't make sense, Rudy. Not if it's what I think it is.'

'That's what it is. Exactly what you'd figured for me.'

'You're wrong, Rudy. I shouldn't have to tell you that. How would I get by at Golie's without you? They're your relatives, and if Carol and I pulled in there by ourselves . . .'

'They'd probably give you a gold watch,' Rudy said sourly. 'Don't kid me, Doc. You think I'm stupid or something?'

'In this case, yes. Perhaps we might get along as well without you, but . . .'

'As well? You'd be a hell of a lot better off, and you know it!'

'I don't agree with you, but let it go. You'll need us, Rudy. Carol and me.'

'Huh-uh. Just a different car, and some other duds. Yeah, and your share of the take. That's all.'

Doc hesitated, looked through the windshield. He glanced at the speedometer. 'Too fast, Rudy. We're liable to pick up a cop.'

'You mean we're ahead of schedule,' Rudy grinned. 'That's what you mean, ain't it?'

'Give Carol the signal, at least. She'll think there's trouble if you don't. Might even lam out on us.'

'Not on you.' Rudy's laugh was enviously angry. 'She'll know you was going to bump me, and . . .'

'No, Rudy. How . . .'

'. . . and she'll figure you got caught in a snarl, so she'll move right on in and try to get you out of it.'

Doc didn't argue the point. In fact, he ceased to argue at all. He simply shrugged, turned around in the seat and was silent.

Coming so quickly, his apparent resignation bothered Rudy. Not because he was afraid Doc had a fast one up his sleeve. Obviously he couldn't have. The feeling came from something else – the irksome, deeply rooted need to justify himself.

'Look, Doc,' he blurted irritably. 'I wasn't burned over what you was going to do to me. You'd've been a sap to do anything else, and I'd be a sap to do anything else. So what's there to cry about?'

'I didn't realize I was crying.'

'And you got no right to,' Rudy said doggedly. 'Look. A hundred and forty in cash. Maybe a hundred and twenty-five out of the bonds. Call it a quarter of a million all together. That ain't no dough in the three-way split – now when it's the last you're going to get and you got to hole up with The King all your life. He doesn't put out anything without cash on the line, and plenty of it.'

'Exactly.' Doc smiled witheringly. 'So it would be an excellent idea not to simply live up your cash, wouldn't it? To use it in such a way that you'd be sure of a generous income as long as you lived.'

'How you mean?' Rudy waited. 'Like startin' a tamale parlor, huh?' he jeered. 'Or maybe a gambling casino?' He waited again. 'You're goin' to run competition with The King?'

Doc laughed softly. The laugh of an adult at a small child's antics. 'Really, Rudy. In your case, I'd suggest a circus. You could be your own clown.'

Rudy scowled and licked his lips uncertainly. He started to speak, stopped himself. He cleared his throat and made another attempt.

'Uh, what'd you have in mind, Doc? Dope, maybe? Smuggling? I figured them things was sewed up, but – ah, to hell with you, Doc! I'm holding aces and you're trying to buy out with hot air.'

'Fine, so why don't we let it go at that?' Doc said easily.

Rudy's foot eased up on the gas. Two emotions warred within him, ingrained suspicion and inherent terror of being in want. Doc was conning him – or was he? Would a smoothie like Doc go out on a limb unless he saw a better one to grab? And – and what did a guy do when he ran out of dough, and he couldn't take it away from someone else?

'You ain't got a thing, Doc,' he mumbled. 'You got something, what you got to lose by telling me about it?'

'Very little – but what would you have to gain? Take such a simple matter as Mexico's foreign policy, its relations, I should say, on a global basis, as compared to those of its Latin-American neighbors. The situation isn't going to change any. Or if it does, it will be to a still more favorable position. It's tied directly to the monetary market – the foreign exchange rate, to use the more popular term – and with inflationary tendencies being what they are, and with gold staked at thirty-five dollars an ounce, the potential for the right kind of operator is . . .'

Doc let his voice trail away. 'Never mind, Rudy,' he said pleasantly. 'It seems simple enough to me, but I didn't really expect you to understand. It's something that's confused a great many highly intelligent people, men who were very successful in their own particular professions.'

'Like double-talk maybe?' Rudy scoffed. But he said it rather feebly. There were certain words, phrases, that rang a bell in his mind. Foreign exchange – inflationary tendencies – monetary market. The terms were identified with news stories which he invariably skipped over, but he guessed they probably meant heavy sugar to a lot of people.

'Like double-talk,' Doc was saying. 'Yes, that's

exactly the way it would sound to you. And I can't say that I blame you a bit. It would probably sound the same way to me if I hadn't spent most of my last four-year stretch reading up on it.'

'Well . . .'

'No, it's no use, Rudy,' Doc said firmly. 'I wish I could. It's a good deal – and a perfectly legitimate one – and you'd have been just the right man to hold down one end of it. But I can't make it any clearer than I have, so there's nothing more to be said.'

Rudy was not a fast thinker – if the weird processes of his mind could be called thinking. But when he made a decision, he made it fast. Abruptly he dropped the gun into his pocket and said, 'All right, Doc. I'm not buying just yet, but I'll take an option.'

Doc nodded. He didn't trust himself to speak.

'I'm keeping your gun,' Rudy went on. 'I'm taking any iron that Carol has when she shows. We stop at night, you two get tied up. We stop for grub or something during the day, one of you stays with me. Either one of you tries anything, that'll be it. Know what I mean? Okay?'

'I know exactly what you mean,' Doc purred, 'and naturally it's okay.'

They crossed a bridge over a small creek. Immediately on the other side, Rudy turned the car straight down the road's embankment, then down the bank of the creek. The wheels bounced high in the air; the steering wheel jerked and spun in his hands. Rudy fought it around to his left, heading the car up the rocky bed of the stream with its shallow trickles of water. A couple of hundred yards farther on, beneath a cloaking arbor of trees, he brought it to a stop.

Doc took a handerkchief from his pocket, mopped at his forehead. He said mildly that he was afraid his neck was broken.

Rudy laughed. Doc got out of the car and removed his hat, continuing the mopping process as Rudy climbed out.

'You kill me, y'know, Doc?' Rudy was still snorting over the joke. 'You really slay me sometimes. I . . .'

'So what's wrong with that?' Doc said. And as Rudy burst into renewed laughter, he took a gun from his hat and fired.

'Got him right through the heart,' Doc told Carol. 'One of those very rare instances where a man actually died laughing.'

'Just so he died.' Carol grimaced. 'That's one character I could never feel easy around. I always had a feeling that he was just about ready to jump at me from the one side I wasn't watching.'

'Alas, poor Rudy,' Doc murmured. 'But how have you been, my dear – to move from the ridiculous to the sublime?'

'We-el – ' Carol slanted a sultry glance at him. 'I think I'll be a lot better tomorrow. You know. After I get a good night's sleep.'

'Tut, tut,' said Doc. 'I see you're still a very wicked young woman.'

They had driven through Beacon City, commenting wonderingly on the smoke, looking curiously at the milling throngs; and now they were far down the highway on the other side of town. Doc was driving, since Carol had driven all night. She sat sidewise in the seat, facing him, her legs curled under her.

Their eyes kept meeting. They kept smiling at each other. Doc patted one of her small round flanks, and she held his hand for a moment, gripping it almost fiercely.

'What are you worried about, Doc?'

'Worried?'

'I can always tell. Is it Golie's? You think that if Rudy isn't with us . . .'

Doc shook his head. 'No trouble there. I wouldn't say I was worried about anything. Just puzzled in a troubled sort of way about our friend Beynon.'

'Oh,' said Carol. 'Oh, yeah.'

Beynon was an attorney, the chairman of the pardon and parole board. Doc's pardon had been bought from him, and there was still fifteen thousand dollars due on the purchase price. He owned a tiny ranch up in the far corner of the state. A bachelor, he lived on it when he was not occupied with some legal case or his official duties. They were going there now.

'Doc—' Carol was staring through the windshield. 'Let's make a switch. Head right into Mexico from here.'

'We couldn't do it, baby. It's too obvious. We're too close.'

'But you haven't been connected with the job. With any kind of break at all, it'll be days before you are.'

'That doesn't help much. Not when the job's this big and this close to the border. They'll have road blocks up fifty miles this side of El Paso. Everyone'll get a shakedown. Anyone trying to cross over had better be strictly clean and able to prove it, or he's in the soup.'

'Well – but the other way, Doc. Beynon is miles off our route, and if you think he may be up to something, why – why . . .'

'Skip him?' Doc gave her a thoughtful look. 'Is that what you were going to suggest, Carol?'

'Why not? What could he do about it?'

Doc smiled wryly, almost irritated with her. Leave Beynon holding the sack for this fifteen thousand? A man with his connections who knew as much about them as he did? It was too preposterous to discuss. They were due at his ranch just as quickly as they could get there from Beacon City, and they had damned well better not dally along the way.

'What could he do?' Carol repeated stubbornly. 'Why pay him off, if he's going to make trouble anyway?'

'I don't know that he is. If he's planning to, however, and if I can't talk him out of it –' Doc left the sentence unfinished, his shrewd eyes thoughtful behind the obscuring sunglasses.

Beynon hadn't run according to form. What he had done was completely out of character, and having acted in such a way, he must have a motive which did not appear on the surface.

Doc stroked his jaw, shook his head absently.

'How did he add up to you, Carol?' he asked. 'I mean aside from the fact that he's an ambitious man with plenty of uses for money. Did he do or say anything that would indicate why he would go for a deal like this one?'

Carol didn't answer him. Doc was about to repeat the question when he saw that she was asleep.

CHAPTER FIVE

Doc went to New York the spring that he graduated from his school, a few weeks after his father's death. He was too young to hold political office, and there were no worthwhile jobs in the town. On the other hand, he was convinced, as were his countless friends, that he would be virtually able to pick and choose from the many opportunities available in a large city.

Things didn't work out that way. He had no difficulty in getting jobs, even in those times of economic depression. But he held none of them more than a few weeks. He was a disrupting influence, throwing any establishment he went into out of kilter. Other employees tended to gather around him, leaving their work undone. Minor supervisors coddled and favored him, to the detriment of morale. As an upper-echelon executive, he would have been invaluable to any company. But he qualified neither in years nor experience for anything but the lowliest jobs. And in that capacity he was simply a nuisance.

Working briefly and rarely, he lived largely on

51

credit and small loans. He worried about these obligations (you did not let down your friends, his father had taught him), and he readily acquiesced when a bar owner-creditor offered to wipe the slate clean, and even gift him with a small bonus, in return for a 'little favor'.

The favor was done; the barkeep collected on his burglary insurance. A few days later he introduced Doc to the proprietor of a floating crap game – a man who needed big money in a hurry and could not depend on gambling to get it. Doc was glad to cooperate with him. He stuck up the game, with some subtle assistance from the proprietor, and they split the proceeds.

Later on, the gambler having introduced him to some 'right' boys, Doc stuck up one of his games again, without prearrangement and without splitting. Nor did this in any way violate his father's code about friendship. On the contrary, the elder McCoy had believed that a man's best friend is himself, that a non-friend was anyone who ceased to be useful, and that it was more or less a moral obligation to cash in any persons in this category, whenever it could be done safely and with no chance of a kick-back.

Doc was made for crime, the truly big operations which he rapidly moved into. No one could get on the inside of a job as easily as he, no one could plan so shrewdly, no one was so imperturbable and cool-headed.

He liked his work. Beginning a stiff prison sentence at age twenty-five he still remained loyally committed to it. His take for the last five years had been more than a hundred thousand a year. For that kind of money, a man could afford to sit it out for a while. He could use his enforced leisure to relax, make new contacts, improve his criminal knowledge and plan new jobs.

Doc's ensuing eight years behind bars were entirely comfortable and often highly enjoyable. After all, a prison cannot function without the cooperation of its inmates; it cannot do so satisfactorily at least, or for very long. So a man who can lead his fellow prisoners, who can deliver their cooperation or withhold it, can get almost anything he asks for. And about the only deprivation Doc suffered was the loss of his income.

Given the same circumstances, he could have taken his second and last prison sentence as lightly as he had the first. But the circumstances differed crucially. He was married – and to a woman almost fourteen years his junior. And he was thirty-six years old.

Doc didn't fret about the situation. He never missed a meal, nor a night's sleep, nor spent a moment in futile regret. He had just one problem – to get out before getting out became pointless. Very well then, if that was what had to be done, he would do it.

He had left sixty thousand dollars on the outside with Carol. With that, and a topflight criminal lawyer, he managed to get his twenty-year sentence reduced to ten. It was a long step on the road to freedom; barring upsets, he would qualify for parole in approximately seven years. But that wasn't good enough for Doc. The seven years might as well be seventy as he saw it. And he wanted no more paroles. Trying to operate while on parole was what had put him where he was.

There were four members of the pardon and parole board, in addition to its chairman, Beynon. Exercising his unusual privileges, Doc approached them one by one. The middle-aged woman member fell for him; he was able to buy her with conversation. The three men members were open to a cash proposition.

Unfortunately Doc had run very, very low on money. He didn't have nearly the amount needed for the three-man buy. And his lawyer, who was usually open to a 'good' proposition himself, refused to play banker. 'Not that I don't trust you, Doc,' he explained. 'I know I'd get mine right off the top of your first job. The point is there wouldn't be any job, because there ain't going to be any pardon. You'd've talked this over with me in the first place, I'd've told you you were wasting your time.'

'But I'd have four members. A majority of the board.'

'Majority, schmority! Three of 'em are crooks, and the gal's a well-meaning imbecile. Beynon would veto them. If they tried to crowd him, he'd start swinging. Kick up such a stink that you'd probably have to do the rest of your time in the hole.'

'Turn it around then. If they can't push him,

can he push them?'

'He *could*. He could make 'em do a skirt dance on the capitol steps if he took a notion. But lay off, Doc. He didn't get that way by going for the fast dollar.'

'Good for him. The better the reputation, the less the risk.'

'Yeah?' The lawyer smiled bitterly. 'Like to meet a guy that almost got disbarred for offering Beynon a cigar? Well, shake hands.'

Doc wasn't convinced. He'd dealt with Honest Johns before, and they'd never turned out as pure as they were supposed to be. So he arranged to see Beynon alone – and that was about all he did. Just saw him. And excused himself as quickly as he could. He was too shrewd – too able an interpreter of a man's expression, the tone of his voice, his overall attitude – to do anything else. Beynon obviously wanted him to make the bribe attempt. It was also obvious that he had some very unpleasant plans for Doc as soon as it was made.

'So I'll have to think of something else,' Doc told Carol on her next visit. 'I don't know what it will be, but Beynon's definitely out.'

'Maybe not. We can't be sure unless we try.'

'I'm sure. Beynon won't take.'

'You mean he never has,' Carol persisted. 'He won't take from you or the lawyer. Ordinarily he wouldn't take from me. But suppose I'd broken up with you, Doc – that it looked like I had. Then he'd have a double out for himself in case anyone got nasty. If I were through with you, then naturally I wouldn't be giving him a bribe. And when a man's wife quits him, it's supposed to be punishment. Don't you see, Doc? I wouldn't have any reason to bribe him, and he *would* have a reason for giving you a break.'

It sounded pretty flimsy to Doc. But Carol wanted to try; and it was pressing four years since he had entered the penitentiary. So he told her to go ahead.

Two months passed before he saw her again. No one could have been more surprised than he when she reported success. Beynon would sell him a pardon. The price five thousand cash, fifteen thousand within ninety days.

News of the robbery had been on the air since ten-thirty that morning. Carol and Doc listened to it, the radio turned to a whisper, as they ate lunch at a roadside drive-in.

Rudy had been identified from rogues' gallery photographs. Except for Jackson, whom he had killed, there was no mention of a confederate. Rudy had robbed the bank. Rudy had driven boldly out of town with 'more than three hundred thousand dollars in swag.' The authorities were 'puzzled' as to how he had gained entry into the bank to kill the guard. But no one raised the question as to whether he *had* shot Wingate.

That would happen in about two days, Doc mused, as he turned the car back into the highway. The trajectory of the bullet, and the bullet

56

itself, would instigate inquiries about 'an unnamed businessman who had been vacationing in Beacon City'. And in two or three more days the businessman would be named, along with his 'business'. But by that time it wouldn't matter.

The news broadcast ended, gave way to a disc jockey. Carol started to doze again, and Doc leaned over to switch off the radio. Then, abruptly, he turned it up. And he and Carol listened silently, tensely, to a late news bulletin.

It was over in a moment. Carol turned the switch, turned slowly, wide-eyed, toward Doc.

'Doc . . .?'

Doc hesitated then shook his head firmly. 'Huh-uh. After all, it happened almost sixty miles away from Beacon City. It couldn't have anything to do with . . .'

'Why couldn't it? Who else would do a thing like that?'

'Anyone could have. Some drunk that lost his head. Some gun-happy teenager.'

'You don't really believe that, Doc. I know you don't,' Carol said. 'You didn't kill him. Rudy's still alive.'

Aimed straight at the heart, Doc's bullet felled Rudy Torrento like a streak of lightning. He stopped breathing, all conscious movement. His eyes glazed, his wedge-shaped face became a foolish, frozen mask, and he crumpled silently backward, an idiot doll cast aside by its master.

The back of his head struck against a rock in

the bed of the stream. The impact deepened and extended his deathlike state. So, far from giving him a second bullet, Doc McCoy hardly gave him a second glance.

And less than thirty minutes after Doc's departure, Rudy came to life again.

His head ached horribly, and his first move was to roll on his stomach and batter the offending rock with his fists. Then memory returned and terror surged through him, and he hurled himself to his feet, clawing. Clawing off his coat and holster. Ripping open his shirt and undershirt. Ripping aside their bloody mess, and seeing and feeling – seeing-feeling – the scarlet frightful-ness of his flesh.

He snarled, whimpered, whined. All silently, his vocal cords constricted. He threw back his head and let out a long, silent howl; shiver-ing, heart-breaking cry of a dying animal. That was taken care of then; the last ceremony which instinct demanded. Now he could begin the actual business of dying. He breathed more and more rapidly. Feverish, poison-filled air rushed into his lungs, his heart raced and stuttered, and his body began to jerk and stiffen.

I knew it, he thought dully, almost with his last thoughts. Back there years ago, back when I was just a kid, back as far as I can remember, I knew it'd be like this. Everything gettin' colder and colder, and the darkness getting deeper and deeper, an' – I knew. I KNEW!

Knew. The word drummed through his mind,

sending a signal back through the years, through thousands of miles, through the grim gray walls and chilled-steel cages of a maximum security prison. And back through time and distance came a voice which told Rudy the Piehead, one of the nation's top ten public enemies, that he was a foolish little child who knew nothing whatsoever.

Rudy blinked, and a little color came back into his fish-gray face. 'Max – ?' he whispered hopefully. 'You – you here, Max?'

'But of course I am. Where else would I be, when my leetle poy Rudy is in trouble? Now, do vot I tell you, instanter!'

Rudy did so. He was quite alone, needless to say; alone with the whispering, half-dry stream and the deep shadows of the arching trees, and the salt-sweet smell of his own blood. But in his mind he was not alone. With him was the one person he had ever loved, or been loved by. Little Max. Herr Doktor Max. Max Vonderscheid, MD, PhD, Psych D – abortionist, physician to criminals; a man who had never been able to say no to a need, regardless of laws and professional ethics.

He and Rudy had been cellmates for three years. Those years, in a so-called tough jug, had given the Piehead the only true happiness he had ever known. One does not forget such things, or such a man. Each of his actions, his words, becomes a thing to treasure.

Rudy stretched out flat on the ground, closed

his eyes, relaxed as completely as he could, and held his breath for a moment. Then he began to count slowly, 'One – two – three –' exhaling and inhaling in time with the count. When he had counted to ten three times, his breathing was near normal and his heart had ceased its wild palpitating. He kept his eyes shut, waiting, and the voice spoke to him again.

He had done well – oh, but werry goot! He had remembered that shock was the big killer; shock first, infection second. If one gave way to shock, even a very minor wound could prove fatal.

'But, Max –' Rudy knew a momentary return of panic. 'It ain't minor! He wasn't ten feet away, and he shot me straight through the . . .'

Rudy sat up. A hoarse laugh welled in his throat. Shot through the ticker? Why, hell if that had happened he wouldn't be alive! He examined his torso again, wondering just what had happened and how.

The riddle remained one to an extent; rather, it had a bit of miracle mixed up in it. The metal-sheathed tip of the holster had obviously deflected the bullet ever so slightly, while it had been further deflected by the iron-hard botch of broken bones and cartilage that formed his rib cage. But still he was very lucky to be alive. And the wound was still nothing to laugh off.

Extending from a point immediately over his heart, the flesh had been furrowed bone-deep across his chest and halfway around the left side of his body. Probably because of the way he had fallen – his chest arching against his clothes and holster strap – he had bled relatively little, much less at any rate than he normally would have. But movement had opened the wound wide now, and he was losing blood at a dangerous rate.

He made a bandage with his undershirt, binding it tight with his belt and holster strap. That helped, but not much; nor did it help much more when he added his socks and handkerchief to the bandage. He had one thing left – two things rather – readily available for putting over the wound. The two thick sheafs of bills he had sequestered from the bank loot. But if he used them, got them bloody – and they probably wouldn't do a damned bit of good anyway . . .

Huh-uh. He had to keep that dough. As long as he had dough and a gun and a car – but above all, the dough – well, he had a chance. To live. To catch up with Doc and Carol. Beyond that – catching up with and killing them – he couldn't think at the moment. It seemed both a means and an end to him. In their deaths, somehow, he would find life for himself.

He climbed weakly into the car and gunned the motor, sending the vehicle roaring up and out of the creek bed and onto the road in a skidding series of jumps and jounces. It was the way it had to be. He lacked the strength for reconnoitering, the strength and the time. All he could do was come up fast, and hope for the best.

His luck held; no one was passing on the road. Luck continued with him as he skirted Beacon

City's outer streets and took to the highway again on the other side. Then swiftly, with his blood, it began to flow away.

He fumbled in the glove compartment of the car, took out a half-filled pint of whiskey. He took a cautious drink, then feeling warmed and stronger, a bigger one. He capped the bottle with one hand, dug cigarettes from his pocket. He found one that was still usable and lit up, drawing the smoke deep into his lungs. Suddenly, for no reason – except that he was drunk – he guffawed.

Laughing, he took another drink, another long puff on the cigarette. Abruptly the bottle fell from his hand, and the car swerved crazily toward the ditch.

The cigarette saved him. As he fought to avoid the ditch, he jammed the burning butt between his palm and the steering wheel, and the pain screamed his mind awake, gave it the complete alertness that it needed. But it began to fade almost as soon as it came. He was conscious; then surely, swiftly, he was losing consciousness again.

'Foolish Rudy. So little blood he has, and he mixed that with alcohol!'

Rudy brought the car to a weaving stop. Awkwardly, gasping with weakness, he raised and turned himself in the seat, reached down onto the rear floor. His fingers found what they were seeking. Closing them with shaky tightness, he flopped down into the seat again.

The two sandwiches were dry and stale. The coffee in the vacuum bottle was cold and tasted sour. But Rudy consumed all of it, and all the food.

Had to eat when you were losing blood. Had to pack the chow down to come off a jag. Had to – had to . . .

Had to get to a doctor.

He was driving again. He could not remember starting up, but the wind was whipping into his face and the highway was leaping madly beneath the car.

'D-doctor,' he mumbled drowsily. 'Got tuh hurry'n see a – see Doc an' . . .'

Awareness flooded over him again. He cursed savagely, bitterly, his dark face contorting into a baffled scowl.

How could he go to a doctor? There'd be other people around: patients, a nurse, maybe the guy's wife. And even if he could take care of them and get treated, then what? So, sure, he'd bump off the sawbones as soon as the job was done, but that wouldn't help. Doctors were busy guys. People were calling on them, dropping in on them, and . . .

'Not necessarily, my poy! Not with a certain kind of doctor. Oh, perhaps he would haf calls. But they would be relatively few, and the callers being under no such dire necessity as would prevail in . . .'

Rudy brushed the sweat from his eyes. He began to slacken his speed, to study the occa-

63

sional RFD mailboxes at the side of the highway.

Country doctor? Was that it? Huh-uh. Country docs didn't live in the country. Right in town, same's any other kind. And if one of 'em was killed or missing, the heat'd be on fast. Faster than fast this close to the bank job. Wouldn't take no Eddie Hoover to figure out that – that . . .

The highway began to blur; everything began to blur, to sink into a kind of gray fuzziness. He crouched forward over the wheel, brushing constantly at his eyes. Just before he lost consciousness completely, he turned into a side road.

He could remember doing nothing after that, yet he did a great deal. As much as he would have if he had been fully aware of his reactions. The frightful present no longer existed; he was reborn, free of all fear and the hideous savagery which festered in it. For Little Max was with him. Max Vonderscheid of the leonine head and the dwarfed hunchbacked body. And he was laughing in a way he had never laughed before, or since.

'Aw, haw, haw! Now you're kidding me again, you little old Dutch bugger, you!'

'*But vot iss so funny, my poor paranoid friend? You should read Jonathan Svift. It vill gif you a better perpective.*

'*Vy not? Der schooling has many parallels. Even it might be said that he must know much more of medicine and anatomy than your proud MD. The basic difference? Only that der patients are usually more deserfing and inwariably less demanding.*'

Rudy came back into consciousness as quickly as he had gone out of it.

He was awake – and considerably refreshed – the moment the other car turned into the side road.

He had crouched down on the floorboards before passing out, lying on the seat from the waist up. Thus he could not be seen, unless someone peered directly into the car. And now he remained hidden, making no move except to firm the grip on the gun he had kept in his hand.

No move was necessary. He had already done everything that could be done in just such an emergency. Both windows on the left side were rolled down. The right wheels were parked on the edge of the roadside ditch. The rearview mirror was twisted to an angle which permitted him to see without raising his head.

It was a black-and-white patrol car. There were two men in it, one young, one middle-aged; apparently a rookie and a regular. They got out on opposite sides of the vehicle and started forward that way. Hands on gun butts, they kept well apart from one another. Moving up on the suspect objective from different directions.

This, of course, was and is the proper procedure, never to be deviated from under any circumstances. Due to the way the car was parked, however, it would have been bothersome if not impossible to carry it through. And since the vehicle was obviously empty, it seemed unnecessary.

So after a moment's pause, one of them shrugged and the other laughed, and they came on together. Almost shoulder to shoulder. Just that once they violated regulations.

And a split second after Rudy reared up over the seat, both of them were dead.

He took their guns and ammunition. He whipped his car round in a U-turn, running partly over the older man's body, and took to the highway again.

He knew what he had to do now, and the knowledge gave him strength. It also amused him, and he laughed as he had when Max Vonderscheid gave him the tip which he was now about to use.

Now, wasn't that somethin' though? Who'd ever think of a dodge like that?

Getting yourself fixed up by a vet, a horse doctor!

CHAPTER SIX

Doc McCoy's greatest vice and major virtue was his sureness. He had been right so often and so long that he could not conceive the possibility of being anything else. Genially, he might charge himself with error, good-naturedly accept the blame for another's mistake. But that was just Doc – part of his masquerade. In his heart he was never wrong – never, that is, about anything that really mattered. And to have a doubt raised as to whether he had actually killed Rudy – a thing at once simple yet vital – made him as near to angry as he ever came.

'I'll tell you, Carol,' he said, a trace of fiddle-string tightness in his voice. 'I don't know who shot those two cops. I don't care. All I know is that it was not done by Rudy Torrento.'

'Well – if you say so, Doc. But . . .'

'Look at it this way. I wasn't a great deal farther from Rudy than I am from you. Suppose I decided to plug you right now. Do you think I'd kill you or not?'

Carol laughed uneasily. He was smiling at her;

joking, of course. No one knew better than she how much Doc thought of her, the lengths he was willing to go to for her sake. But if she *hadn't* known – if she *hadn't* been sure that Doc wanted and needed her just as much after the bank robbery as before . . .

The thought nettled her. She spoke in a tone, a manner, that was almost an identical match for his. 'Suppose I decided to plug you right now,' she said, smiling, playful – steady-eyed. 'Do you think I'd kill you or not?'

'I'm sorry,' Doc said warmly. 'To answer your question – I wouldn't blame you if you did exactly like that.'

'I don't like being shut up, Doc. I don't intend to be.'

'And you're quite right, my dear.'

'So don't talk to me that way again. Never, ever, understand? I know you didn't mean it like it sounded, but . . .'

Doc turned the car off onto a country road. Stopping just over the crest of a little hill, he turned silently and took his wife into his arms. He kissed her, drew her more and more tightly to him. He kissed her again, his sure hands pressing and caressing her small hard-soft body.

And afterward, as they drove on, they were again one with each other; each an extension of the other.

Their brief flare-up was forgotten. There was no more mention of Rudy. Carol was glad to be convinced, to be sure that Rudy was dead.

Mostly they were silent, happy and content merely to be together. But as the sun sank lower in the sky, there was more talk of Beynon. The man – his motives, rather – still bothered Doc. It was difficult to believe that the parole chief meant to grab all the bank loot, instead of the relatively small share he had agreed to accept. To think that such a man would commit murder – as he would have to – for any amount of money was nothing short of ridiculous. On the other hand, was it any more ridiculous than his ostensible sellout – at the risk of his career and reputation – for a mere pittance?

Carol was of little help with the riddle. She seemed indifferent to its answer; a little bored, dully withdrawn. Then, a few miles from Beynon's place she brightened, turned almost gaily to her husband. 'I've got an idea, Doc. Let me take Beynon his fifteen grand.'

'You?' Doc gave her a quick glance. 'Without me, you mean?'

'Yes. You take the money satchel, and . . .'

'And just where would I take it to? Where would I wait? At the side of the road, or at one of these little inland villages – some wide place in the road where every stranger gets the big-eye and maybe an interview by the town clown?'

'We can work it out. Please, Doc. What do you say?'

'That I can't believe you're serious,' said Doc evenly. 'I appreciate your concern for me, of course, but – ' he shook his head. 'It just wouldn't do, lamb. As I mentioned before. If Beynon is planning something, we've got to know about it now. We've got to get it settled now.'

'But he wouldn't bring things to a showdown if you were by yourself. In any event, the kind of settlement – if one is necessary – is something I'd want to decide on myself.'

Carol started to say something else, then shrugged and lapsed into silence. Doc lighted a cigarette and extended the package, and she shook her head wordlessly.

They skirted a small village, its church spires poking up through a grove of trees. Doc slowed the car to make a quick study of the road map, then resumed his former speed. A few miles farther on, he turned into a narrow dirt road which stretched ribbonlike up through the hills.

It was less than an hour before sunset now, and a chill southwesterly wind was stirring. Back in the hills, Doc got an occasional glimpse of a ranch house or an outbuilding. He didn't like that. In this isolated area their car could be seen for a very long way, and one as conspicuous as theirs was certain to be remembered.

The trail met with another. At the rutted intersection, two mailboxes stood catercornered to each other. On one of them, crudely printed in black paint, was the name Beynon. Doc stopped the car and looked carefully around the lonely, rolling terrain.

Apparently the intersection was not visible from either of the two houses which must be nearby. He considered this fact, murmuring absently that Beynon's place should be just over the next hill to their right.

Carol responded with a murmur of agreement. Doc scratched his cheek thoughtfully, then reached into the back of the car and lifted the money satchel into the front seat.

He opened it, sorted out fifteen thousand dollars and put it in the inside pocket of his coat. Then, as long as it was something that needed to be done anyway, he gave Carol a few hundred dollars in small bills, stuffed his wallet with a few hundred more, and assembled a third sheaf totaling perhaps a thousand. This was scat money – dough to be kept readily available. Doc fastened it together with two of the bank's paper money bands, laid it in right at the top of the suitcase and closed and locked it again.

Then he got out, unlocked the trunk and put the suitcase inside. He did not lower the trunk lid immediately; instead, catching Carol's eye in the rearview mirror, he gave her a grin and a wink.

'That idea of yours,' he smiled. 'If you don't mind a variation of it, along with a little cramping . . .'

Carol's face lit up. She hopped out of the car and came around to the rear; pulling the gun from her belt, she checked its chamber with two crisp metallic clicks before shoving it back into place. The action sent a frown flickering through Doc's eyes. He laid a hand on her arm as she started to climb into the trunk.

She was to take it very easy, he cautioned. To do nothing without his lead. Beynon was not a killer. He was a very prominent man. And they – she and Doc – had a long way to travel.

Carol nodded that she understood. She climbed into the trunk, and Doc lowered the lid, leaving the lock off the latch.

As he had supposed Beynon's place was only a few hundred yards away, just over the crest of the nearest hill. The house was one of those old-fashioned ranch dwellings, two-storied and painted white, with a long veranda or 'gallery' extending across the front.

Down the slope to the rear of the house was a large red barn, cow partitioned down one side to provide a garage for Beynon's car. Adjoining it was a plank corral, which opened at the far end into a lushly grassed pasture. Grazing in it were a couple of riding horses and a few head of white-faced cattle. Beynon kept no employees; the ranch, if it could be called that, was merely a hobby with him. When business affairs took him away, a neighbor looked after his small amount of livestock.

Doc parked the car in the yard beneath a gnarled cottonwood tree. He got out, casually brushing at his clothes, and looked around. It was very quiet. The big old house, with its shadow-black windows, seemed never to have been occupied. Beynon's car – a three-year-old model – was in the garage, but there was no sign of him.

Doc strolled across the yard, whistling tunelessly, softly. He stepped up on the porch. The front door was opened. Through the screen he called, 'Beynon,' and stood waiting, listening. There was no answer – no sound. But that in itself, the no-sound, the complete silence, was an answer.

Doc opened the screen. He slammed it again – from the outside. Then he stepped down from the porch and strode silently around the house to the back door. It also stood open, and the screen was unlatched. He peered in, eyes squinting against the shadows. With a soft sigh, he walked in.

Beynon sat at the long kitchen table, his head pillowed in his arms. On the checkered oilcloth in front of him was a tipped-over glass, and a half-empty quart bottle of whiskey.

Drunk, Doc thought, with less tolerance than was customary to him. The great man had troubles, so he got drunk.

Picking up a glass from the sink, he walked around the table and sat down opposite the parole chief. He poured himself a drink, took a sip of it, and lighted a cigarette. Deliberately he spewed smoke at the man across from him – it was probably the least startling way of any to wake him up. Beynon's head, with its wild mass of black hair, jerked irritably; then, abruptly, he sat up.

Except for a very faint thickness of speech, he seemed quite sober. Either he had spilled much more of the whiskey than he had drunk, or he had slept it off. His burning, black eyes were clear. They were as contemptuous, as knowing of Doc as they had been back at the prison.

Doc smiled, made a small gesture with his glass. 'I hope you don't mind? It's been a rather trying day.'

'Where's your wife?' Beynon said.

'We're traveling in different cars. She'll be along in an hour or so.'

'How nice of her,' Beynon said in his rich, musical voice. 'How very, very nice of her to come to see me.' He poured himself a drink, threw it down at a gulp. 'Or perhaps she isn't,' he said. 'Perhaps her comings and goings have ceased for all time.'

Doc shrugged idly. 'If you're inferring that I killed her . . .'

'Where's Rudy, McCoy? Where's your friend Torrento? He's in another car, too?'

'Yes. And neither he nor the car is moving in case you're interested. I thought you'd be primarily interested in knowing that I have the bank money in my car.'

This was bait. Beynon didn't rise to it. Doc waved it at him again.

'You've received five thousand dollars from me, from my wife rather. I agreed to pay fifteen thousand more. Frankly—' Doc turned on his sincerest look, 'frankly, I don't think that's enough, Mr Beynon. We didn't get as much out of this job as we hoped to, but that's no fault of yours. And . . .'

'Three people have been killed, so far, McCoy. Whose fault would you say that was?'

'Oh, now—' Doc spread his hands. 'You mustn't feel . . .'

'Car – your wife told me that no one would be killed. She swore to it.'

'I'm sorry. I imagine she was simply trying to spare your feelings. But getting back to the subject . . .'

'It's still murder, McCoy. How many more will there be before all this is over? If it is ever all over. How many more lives will I have on my hands?'

Doc hesitated, started to attempt some soothing comment. Then he leaned forward a little, spoke with abrupt bluntness. Beynon, he said, had best stop fretting about others. He had, or would have, plenty to worry about on his own account. 'It's just a matter of time until the Beacon City job is pinned on me. When it is, the man responsible for my pardon – you, in other words – will have some very tough questions to answer.'

'And there's just one answer for them. That I'm a murderer and a thief.' Beynon looked at him strangely; a dully wondering look. 'So you did anticipate it. You knew exactly what it would cost me. My career, disgrace, disbarment. Maybe a long stretch in prison myself. You knew all that, and yet – yet . . .'

'Now, you're exaggerating the situation,' Doc cut in smoothly. 'You'll have an uncomfortable time of it, but it won't be nearly as bad as that. You've got a lot of friends, a simon-pure reputation. It's an accepted fact that you've never taken a dishonest dime in your life. Under the . . .'

'Never a dime, McCoy?' Beynon laughed thickly. 'You wouldn't say I'd taken about thirty of them?'

'I was saying,' Doc said, 'that under the circumstances you should come through this fine. About the worst you can be charged with is gross bad judgement.'

He paused, frowning slightly as Beynon laughed again. Faintly, almost lost in the night breeze, he heard a metallic squeak. The opening – or perhaps the closing – of the car's trunk.

'Bad judgement,' he repeated, his eyes holding the parole chief's. 'Now, that's not so terrible, is it? It shouldn't be so hard to face considering that instead of fifteen thousand more, you're getting – well – twenty-seven and a half?'

'Twenty-seven and a half, eh?' Beynon nodded gravely. 'Twenty-seven thousand, five hundred just for facing that. And how much do you think I should have, McCoy for facing myself?'

'Nothing,' Doc said. 'Not a damn penny.'

He was tired, weary of coddling Beynon. He saw no reason to. The man wasn't going to do anything rash; he wasn't going to do anything period. He simply wanted to whine – make a big display of the conscience which had been conveniently asleep at the time he had sold out his office.

'You're a crook,' Doc went on. 'A particularly rotten kind. Now, stop fighting the fact. Just accept it and make the most of it. Believe me, you won't find it so bad.'

'I see.' A skull's grin wreathed Beynon's haggard face. 'You see us as two of a kind, is that it?'

'No,' Doc said equably, 'you're much worse than I am. You knew the kind of man I was – and I've never pretended to be any other kind. You knew, if you're not a complete idiot, that I play rough when I think it's necessary. You didn't have to give me a pardon; no one twisted your arm. You did it for money, and damned little of it at that. The kind of money that – yes?'

Beynon's grin widened. He said softly. 'Now, aren't you mistaken about that, McCoy? Wasn't there another factor involved, and did I have a choice?'

'I don't know what it would be.'

'No,' Beynon nodded slowly. 'No, you really don't, do you? I was certain that you did, that it was a put-up job. I was convinced of it, despite some very wishful thinking to the contrary. But now – a small drink, Mr McCoy? Or, no, I think the circumstances call for a large one.'

With grave courtesy, he slopped whiskey into Doc's glass. Then he filled his own, pursing his lips sympathetically as Doc brushed the drink aside. 'I don't blame you a bit, sir. Oh, believe me, I understand your feelings. You might say they were identical with my own at one time.'

'I'm in a hurry,' Doc snapped. 'What are you talking about?'

'You still don't see it? Well, perhaps it will help if I mention the word blackmail.'

'Blackmail? What . . .'

'A highly original kind, Mr McCoy. Almost an attractive kind. To elaborate, one is forced to go along with the wishes of the blackmailer, whether or no. But the mailed fist – or should I say the muddy fist? – also contains a prize; something delectable indeed. One is even allowed to sample it generously, by way of making sure that it is worth the cooperation which one is forced to extend . . .'

He let his voice trail away. He waited deliberately, prolonging the delicate torture, deepening the sickish heart-tightening suspense. Then, although nothing more needed to be said, he resumed talking. He spelled the thing out, speaking with a false sympathy that was worse than any hatred. Speaking with lewdly gleaming eyes, his wide mouth salaciously wet.

He's drunk, Doc thought. He's lying. He's sore, so he's striking back, digging at the one spot where it will hurt.

In the whispering twilight there was a minutely exploratory movement of the screen door. His attention riveted on Beynon, Doc didn't hear it.

'Take it a little at a time,' Beynon was saying. 'Approach the matter from all sides. One—' he held up a finger, waggled it in pseudo-courtroom fashion. 'One, we have an extremely attractive woman, one who has thoroughly demonstrated her desirability. Two—' he put up a second finger, 'we have the woman's husband, probably the most skillful bank robber in the country, who is serving a long prison sentence. Three—' another finger, 'we have a powerful politician, a man who is in a position to free the robber husband. Why should he be freed? Well, naturally, to rob a bank, thus leaving the woman and the politician comfortably fixed for life, the ill winds peculiar to public office notwithstanding. Secondly – would you care to guess at the second – but by no means the lesser – motive, Mr McCoy? No? Very well, then . . .'

His voice purred on, pushing and twisting the knife; moving Doc McCoy off balance, hacking away at the one thing he had trusted and believed in.

'Consider, Mr McCoy. Our robber is notoriously ingenious and deadly. He is also devoted to his wife. If he lost her to another man, he would quite likely kill both of them at the soonest opportunity – at the end of his prison sentence, that is. This didn't appeal to them at all, of course. Yet unless they gave each other up and resigned themselves to a life of modest or no comforts, there was only one alternative. To free the bank robber, let him make them wealthy, and then, having lured him to an isolated spot such as this . . .'

Beynon leaned forward, his voice dropping to a harsh conspiratorial whisper. 'Then, Mr McCoy, when he is off guard, when he is no longer sure of where he stands, whether he is captured or captor, when, being sure, he still would not dare to move; then, Mr McCoy – *kill him!*'

Doc heard the screen at last. Heard it close – firmly, with no attempt at silence.

Out of the corner of his eye, he saw Carol move out of the shadows. And he saw the gun, held very steady, in her hand.

Was it pointed at him? If he moved, would it be pointed at him – blasting him into oblivion before his move could be completed?

It would, he was sure. Carol was practical. She could be as merciless as he. Undoubtedly she had heard much if not all that Beynon had said. If she thought that he, Doc, believed the man – and was he so hard to believe? Mustn't there be a great deal of truth in what he said – if she thought that he believed Beynon, and was about to act accordingly . . .

He didn't know what to do. With extreme cleverness – or with drunken, conscience-stricken truthfulness – Beynon had so fixed things that any move or no move could be fatal.

'This – this is stupid,' he said, his voice amused but deeply sincere; making the words at once a statement and a plea. 'Did you really think I'd fall for a sucker pitch like that?'

'A trick question,' Beynon pointed out promptly. 'You don't know whether it is or isn't a sucker pitch. To be fair, neither do I. Obviously, I believed little Carol – our Carol, shall I say? – at one time. But with three men killed in spite of her promise that there would be none – well, was just that one promise of hers a lie or were all of them? Another thing . . .'

'That's enough,' Doc broke in. 'It was a good try, Beynon, but . . .'

'Another thing—' Beynon raised his voice. 'She may have been entirely sincere and truthful with me. It may be that she just didn't know there would be three murders – in addition, of course, to your own. But seeing my dismay at the killings, and fearful that I might be a frail reed to tie to . . .'

It was wicked, cruel. And still he wasn't through. Beaming falsely, he drove home the final nail in Doc's cross of doubt.

'Carol, sweetheart—' Beynon pushed back his chair and stood up, extended one arm in an embracing gesture. 'I hope you won't think ill of her, Mr McCoy. After all, you were locked up for a long time – your first separation since your marriage, wasn't it? – and she's a healthy, vigorous young woman with perhaps more than her share of . . .'

Carol let out a low moan. She came at him with a rush, and jammed the gun into his stomach. And the room rocked with its stuttering explosions.

Beynon shrieked wildly; it sounded strangely like laughter. He doubled at the waist, in the attitude of a man slapping his knees; then collapsed, dead, riddled with bullets, before his body completed its somersault.

The gun dropped from Carol's fingers. She

stood very straight, eyes squeezed shut, and wept helplessly.

'He-he was lying, Doc. The mean, h-hateful, dirty—! I wish I could kill him again . . .!'

'There, there now. Don't let it throw you.' Doc held her in his arms, caressed her with hands that were still damp with sweat. 'I'll get you a drink of the booze here, and . . .'

'He *was* lying, Doc! Y-you believe me, don't you? There wasn't anything at all like – like he said.'

'Of course there wasn't,' Doc said warmly. 'I never thought for a moment that there was.'

'I – I was just friendly. J-just pretended to be. I couldn't help it. I had to be nice, make him want to know me, or he wouldn't have . . .'

It was a moment before Doc realized that she was talking about only the one facet of Beynon's story: her supposed or actual infidelity. That was all that bothered her, all that she was denying. Which must mean that there was nothing else to deny.

It was a comforting thought, and he hugged her to him fiercely with a kind of shamed ardor. Then he realized that if the undisputed part of the story was false, the other must be true. And he had to fight to keep from shoving her away.

'Th-that's why I didn't want to come here'. Doc. I-I was afraid he'd say something – m-make up a lot of lies, just to get even with me, and . . .'

Doc sat down on a chair and pulled her onto his

lap. Smiling lovingly, he got her to take a drink, gently dried her tears with his handkerchief.

'Now, let's look at it this way,' he said. 'You wanted to get me out. The only way you could do it was to compromise him, so – wait, now! There had to be something between you. After all, if you didn't have a club to swing over his head, how . . .'

He broke off. The look in her eyes stopped him. He forced a laugh which sounded reasonably genuine, then stood up, lifting her in his arms.

'A very clever man,' he smiled. 'It's hard not to admire him. But I think we've let his gag bother us enough, so suppose we forget it?'

Carol brightened a little. 'Then you do believe me, Doc?'

'Believe you?' Doc said warmly. 'Now, why wouldn't I believe you, my dear?'

He carried her upstairs and laid her down on a bed. She clung to his hand when he started to straighten, made him sit down at her side while she told him how she had compromised Beynon. It sounded reasonable. Doc seemed satisfied. Urging Carol to try to rest, he went back downstairs and lugged Beynon's body down into the basement.

It was the work of a few minutes to bury the corpse in the coal bin. Afterward he stood at the corner sink, scrubbing his hands and arms with gritty mechanics' soap, drying them on a handful of waste cloth. Then, lost in thought, he remained where he was, a brooding shadow in the near blackness of the basement.

Carol. Why couldn't he accept her explanation? Beynon was a hard drinker at times. Carol had had to call at his apartment to talk to him. So, playing upon his weakness, she had got him so drunk that he passed out. And he was still dead to the world early the next morning when she slipped out of the place. That was all she had had to do, except, of course, to make sure that she was seen coming and going by the elevator operator and desk clerk. That was all – more than enough. For a man of Beynon's prominence – the head of the state's pardon and parole board – to have the wife of a notorious criminal in his apartment for an all-night stay . . .

Nothing else was necessary, so doubtless nothing else had taken place. As for the bribe money – well, as long as Beynon was stuck, there was no point in refusing a bit of salve.

It all fitted, Doc thought. Yet piece by piece, item by item, he could knock it apart. His mind moved around and around in a circle, disbelieving each time it was on the point of believing.

He was ready to admit that his shaky faith was a personal thing. As a professional criminal, he had schooled himself against placing complete trust in anyone. And as a criminal, he had learned to link infidelity with treachery. It revealed either a dangerous flaw in character, or an equally dangerous shift in loyalties. In any case, the woman was a bad risk in a game where no risk could be tolerated.

So . . .

Abruptly, Doc broke the agonizing circle of his thoughts. He stood off from himself, standing this fretful, teetering creature that he was now alongside the suave, sure and unshakable Doc McCoy; and the comparison made him squirm.

Now, no more of this, he lectured himself; he smiled softly. No more, either now or later.

Carol had mopped up the kitchen. Now she was at the oil stove, measuring coffee into an enamel pot. Doc walked over to her and put his arms around her. She turned hesitantly, a little fearfully, and looked up into his face.

Doc kissed her enthusiastically. He said mock-seriously, 'Madam, were you aware that you had a damn fool for a husband?'

'Oh, Doc! Doc, honey!' She clung to him, burying her face against his chest. 'It's my fault. I wanted to tell you the truth right back in the beginning, but . . .'

'But you were afraid I'd react exactly the way I did,' Doc said. 'That coffee smells good. How about some sandwiches to go with it?'

'All right. But shouldn't we be beating it out of here, Doc?'

'Well,' Doc grinned wryly, 'of course, I wouldn't recommend an indefinite stay. But there's no great rush that I can see.' He sauntered over to the refrigerator, peered inside and lifted out a butt of baked ham. 'Beynon wouldn't have known exactly when we'd show up. Therefore, he'd have made sure that no one else dropped in on him tonight.'

'I guess I shouldn't have killed him, should I, Doc? It's going to make things tough for us.'

Doc laid plates and silver on the table. He set out butter and bread. He said that Beynon's death was regrettable but unavoidable; when an accessory to a crime collapsed so completely, there was nothing to do but kill him. 'I don't know just how tough it'll make things for us. Maybe not at all. But it certainly forces us to change our plans.'

Carol nodded, and lifted the coffee from the stove. 'Want to put the cream on for me, honey?' she said; then, 'just how will it change them?'

'Well, here's the way I add it up.' Doc sat down at the table, and carved meat onto their plates. 'Our car must have been spotted on the way up here. At least we have to assume that it was. Still playing it safe, we can't rule out the possibility that someone got a look at us. Maybe some kid stalking a rabbit near the road, or a nosy housewife with time on her hands and a pair of binoculars . . .'

'It could happen,' Carol agreed. 'We change out of these duds, then. Leave our car here and take Beynon's.'

'Right. We try to make it appear that the three of us have gone off somewhere together, and that we'll be coming back. But—' Doc took a sip of his coffee, 'Here's where the rub comes in. We don't know what Beynon's plans were, his appointments. For all we know he may have been due to see or call someone tomorrow

86

morning, or someone may have been scheduled to see or call him here. Then there's the livestock – that's the real tip-off. When Beynon shows up missing, without having notified his part-time hired hand—' Doc shook his head. 'We'll have to get off the road. We can't risk it a moment longer than we absolutely have to.'

'No, we can't, can we?' Carol frowned. 'We hole up with someone, then?'

'What gave you that idea? Who would we hole up with?'

'Well, I just thought that if – weren't you supposed to have a good friend out this way? Somewhere near Mexico, I mean? You know, that old woman – Ma Santis.'

Doc said, regretfully, that he didn't have. Ma Santis was on the other side of Mexico, the Southern California side. At least, it had been rumored that she was there, although no one seemed to know where. 'I don't know that she's even alive, but it's my guess that she probably isn't. When you get as well known as Ma Santis and her boys, people have you cropping up around the country for years after you're dead.'

'Well. If there's no place for us to hole up . . .'

'I think we'd better be moving.' Doc pushed back his plate and stood up. 'We can talk about it while we're getting ready.'

They cleared up the dishes and put them away. They changed into conservative clothes. As for talk – a discussion of their plans – there was very little. The decision was made for them.

One saw it as readily as the other. They had to travel far faster than they had planned, and it was unsafe to use the highways. So there was only one thing they could do.

Aside from putting the kitchen to rights and smoothing out the upstairs bed, they did nothing to expunge the signs of their brief presence in the house. Doc did suggest that they wipe everything off to remove their fingerprints, but that was a joke and Carol grinned dutifully. Criminals are not nearly so cautious about fingerprints as is popularly supposed. Not, at least, the big-time operators who treat crime as a highly skilled profession. They know that an expert fingerprint man might work all day in his own home without picking up an identifiable set of his own prints. They also know that fingerprints are normally only corroborative evidence; that they will probably be tabbed for a certain crime, and the alarm set to ringing for them, long before they are tied to the job by fingerprints – if they ever are.

Doc filled Beynon's car with gasoline from a drum in the garage, also filling two five-gallon cans which he put in the rear of the car. He drove the car out into the yard, and Carol drove the convertible inside, and then they were on their way.

A couple of hours driving got them off of the county roads and back onto the highway. They paused there briefly to consult their road maps, picking out the most practical route to Kansas City. The town was far to the north, farther rather than nearer their ultimate destination. But that, of course, was its advantage. It was the last place they would be expected to go. As a jumping-off place, it offered no clue as to what their destination might be.

Their plan was to abandon the car at Kansas City and take a train westward. It was not, they knew, an ideal one. You are confined on a train. You are part of a relatively small group, and thus more easily singled out. Still, there was only one alternative – to go by plane – and a train was by far the best bet.

The night was chill, and speeding north it grew colder. In the heaterless car Carol shivered and snuggled close to her husband. He patted her protectively, remarked that it was a shame they had had to give up the convertible. 'It was a nice car. I imagine you put a lot of thought into picking it out, didn't you?'

'Oh, well—' Carol's small shoulder shrugged against his. 'It was nice of you to say that, Doc,' she added. 'Even to think about me being disappointed or uncomfortable at a time like this.'

Doc said it was nothing at all; it came perfectly natural to anyone as generally splendid as he. Carol reproved him with a delicate pinch.

They rode cozily shoulder to shoulder, and somehow, despite the dropping temperature, the car seemed to grow warmer. Carol was comfortably pert. Doc was Doc; tender, amusing, restful – exuding the contagious good humor of complete self-confidence.

So it had been on nights past. The good nights (the good seems always to be in the past) before Doc's prison stretch. Just what broke the spell Carol could not have said. But gradually she found herself withdrawing; moving over to her own side of the seat. Gradually she began to study Doc's words, the tone of his voice, the play of expression over his homely-handsome face.

Doc may or may not have noticed the change – may or may not have without knowing which was the case. Characteristically, and up to a point, he did not always allow himself to know what he thought or what he felt. He had come to a decision, decided on a certain course of conduct. If an obstacle could not be circumvented, ignore it. As long as it could be. Or until a better course suggested itself.

A couple of hours before dawn, he refueled the car from the two gas cans. Driving on again, he at last asked Carol if something was troubling her. 'If I've done or said anything . . .'

'You haven't,' she said. 'I suppose that that's – well, never mind. Don't pay any attention to me, Doc.'

'Now, of course, I'll pay attention to you,' Doc said genially. 'Now and at all other times. So let's get this thing straightened out, whatever it is.'

'Well, it's really nothing, but—' she hesitated, laughed with nervous apology. 'I guess it just occurred to me that if you – if you felt a certain way, I probably wouldn't know it.'

'Yes?' His voice tilted upward. 'I'm not sure I understand.'

'I'm talking about Beynon!'

'Beynon?' He gave her a curious look. 'But what's there to say about him? You explained everything. I believed you. It's all settled.'

Silence closed over the car again. They raced through the headlight-tunneled night, and the black walls slapped shut behind them. Time and space were the immediate moment. Behind and beyond it there was only the darkness.

Doc shifted in the seat and got cigarettes out of his pocket. He lighted two of them and passed one to her. And after a time, after it was finished, she drew close to him again.

He drew her a trifle closer. He pulled the tail of his topcoat from beneath him and tucked it over her knees.

'Better?' he asked softly.

'Better,' she nodded. Because it was. It was warmer. Friend or foe, there was at least someone with her, and anything was better than the utter loneliness.

'I understood what you were talking about,' he went on quietly. 'I simply didn't know how to reply to it. Or what to do about it.'

'I know, Doc.'

'It leaves me without a corner to go to. If I'm agreeable, it's pretense. If I'm not, that also is cause for alarm. You see, my dear? You just can't think that way. It's foolish and it's dangerous, and – you do see that, don't you?'

'I see it,' she nodded; and then desperately, with what was almost a cry, 'Then it is all right, Doc? Honestly? You're not sore or suspicious about – anything? Everything's just like it always was?'

'I said so. I've done everything I could to show you.'

'But you might do that anyway! You might act just as sweet as pie, and all the time you'd be planning t-to – to . . .'

'Carol,' said Doc soothingly. 'My poor darling little girl.'

And she sobbed harshly, sighed, and fell asleep against his shoulder.

CHAPTER SEVEN

It was early afternoon when Doc let Carol out of Kansas City's Union Railroad Terminal. Being much the 'cooler' of the two of them – much less likely to be identified – she kept the money satchel with her. While Doc drove away to dispose of the car, she entered the station and headed for the coach ticket windows. At one of them she bought a one-way ticket to Los Angeles. At another, far removed, she bought a second one. Then, hesitantly, with a look at the lobby clock, she again picked up the money bag and her overnight case.

It was almost an hour until train time – Doc had previously checked the schedule by telephone. He wouldn't be showing up until the next to last minute, so she had almost an hour to kill – and to remain in sole custody of approximately two hundred and fifty thousand very hot, very bloody dollars.

She had never faced such nerve-wracking responsibility before. It had had to be hers, but still, with part of her mind, she was resentful that it had been thrust upon her.

She looked around the vaulted lobbby, then, lurching a little from the weight of the bag, she started for the women's rest room. After a dozen steps or so, she set the bag down, started to shift it to her other hand. And in a blur of movement – in her fear and nervousness it seemed a blur – she saw it snatched up from the floor.

It was a redcap, one of several who had so far proferred their services. But at the moment he had no identity for Carol. He was just a hand, an arm, a half-turned back – a something that was about to make off with the bag.

Taking in her expression, he said, 'Hope I didn't startle you, ma'am. Just thought I'd . . .'

'*You give that here!*' With a wild grab, she recovered the satchel. 'You hear me? You give . . .'

'Kind of looks like you already got it, ma'am.' He grinned at her pleasantly. 'Ain't that so? Now, how about letting me check it for you?'

'No!' She backed away from him. 'I mean, I don't want it checked. I j-just . . .'

'Put it on the train for you, then. Mighty heavy bag for a little lady like you to carry.'

'No! And you'd better get away from me, or I'll – I'll . . .'

'Well, yes, ma'am,' he said coldly. 'Yessiree, ma'am!'

Regaining some control of herself, she mumbled a grimacing word of apology. Very conscious that his eyes were following her, she hurried down the vaulted lobby. Her arm ached. She was panting, sweating with exertion. She had a feeling that everyone in the place was watching her, wondering about her.

At long last – after hours, miles, seemingly – she got out of the waiting room proper and into a wing of the building. She paused there gratefully, setting the bag against the wall and resting the toe of one shoe against it.

Her breath came back; she patted the sweat from her face, became cooler, calmer. In a half-resentful way she felt ashamed of herself. There had been no reason for her panic. The bag looked like any other bag. If the police had been alerted, there wasn't a chance in ten thousand they'd be able to spot her. All she had to do was follow Doc's instructions: stay in the crowd, keep the bag with her at all times, carry it onto the train herself. It was simple enough. It was what she knew she should do, without being told by Doc. But . . .

No buts. It was what she had to do. Checkroom attendants were always losing things. Handing them out to the wrong people, banging bags around until they flew open. There were similar risks in dealing with redcaps, baggage porters. Nothing ever happened, naturally, to a two-dollar suitcase with a few bucks' worth of clothes in it. But let the bag contain something hot – money or jewelry or narcotics, or part of a dismembered corpse – and sure as shootin' there was a foul-up.

It happened all the time. You needed only

to read the newspapers to know that it did.

Doc had been fearful that the bag would be too heavy for her. She had lifted it, assured him that she could manage it. She had also assured him – and pretty shortly at that – that her nerves were equally up to the job. But that had been then, and somehow everything had changed since then. The sureness which she had felt with him had melted away; and suddenly, with a spur of panic, she knew why.

Not only had she never faced any such responsibility as this before, she had never faced any that remotely approached it. Nothing of do-or-die importance; nothing without Doc to guide her and work with her. She had thought that she had; Doc had tactfully let her think so. But invariably they had been a team. The one thing she had swung on her own was the Beynon deal; and that obviously, and regardless of the consequences, was something that would have been a lot better left unswung.

Actually, she hadn't been around very much. She was virtually untraveled. Until she met Doc, she'd never been out of her hometown. Since then, there'd been considerable travel by car, but she'd made only one train trip in her life.

She wasn't used to railroad stations. Even without the money bag she would have felt some unsureness.

Which I'd damn well better get over, she thought grimly. If Doc caught me acting like this, standing off in a corner by myself . . .!

He wouldn't like it. Far too much had already happened that he didn't like.

Resolutely, she picked up the bag and started back to the waiting room. The resolution lasted for a few steps, and then she began to slow, to hesitate. If only she could get rid of the thing for a few minutes. Long enough to make sure that she hadn't been spotted; to get a drink, to clean up a little. The drink, particularly, she needed. A good stiff jolt to pull her together again and . . .

She heard a dull clang of metal against metal; jumped a little, her eyes swerving toward it. But it was only someone slamming the door of a baggage locker. She started to move on toward the waiting room, and then her heart did a little skip-jump of relief, and she swung almost gaily toward the row of lockers on the other side of the wing.

She would be taking no chance in leaving the bag in a private locker. Doc couldn't object to it – in fact, he didn't even need to know about it. She could recover the bag before he showed up at the station.

She crossed the marble-paved foyer, set down the satchel and overnight case. She got a quarter out of her purse and stooped in front of an empty locker. Frowning, she sought in vain for the coin slot. Straightening again, she had started to read the metal instruction plate when a young man sauntered by. A young-oldish man with a small brown mustache and prematurely graying hair.

He was neatly dressed, engaging of manner. He would have been handsome except for the slight sharpness of his features.

'Kind of a Chinese puzzle, isn't it?' he said. 'Well, here's how you work it.'

Before Carol could object to the intrusion, he had taken the quarter from her hand, inserted it in the elusive slot and swung open the door. 'Imagine you want to keep the dressing case with you, right?' he smiled. 'Well, in we go with the big boy, then. Now—' he slammed and rattled the door, 'we'll just test this to make sure that it's locked; maybe you'd better test it, too.'

Carol tested it. He handed her a yellow-flanged locker key, courteously brushed aside her thanks, and sauntered off toward the waiting room.

In the station's bar-and-grill ladies' room, Carol touched up her makeup and allowed her suit to be brushed off by the attendant. Then, going out to the bar, she ordered and drank two double martinis. She wanted a third – not the drink itself so much as the excuse it would provide for remaining there. Just to stay there a little longer, where it was cool and shadowed and quiet, and feel the strength and the confidence spread through her. To feel *safe*.

But the hands of the clock pointed forbiddingly. It was barely ten minutes until train time.

Draining the last drop from her glass, she hurried out of the bar. She located her locker, inserted the key and turned it. Or tried to. It wouldn't turn. It didn't fit.

Her stomach cramped convulsively and the two drinks rose up in her throat. Swallowing nauseously, she removed the key and examined it; read the number with bewildered disbelief.

That couldn't be right! She *knew* that the bag had gone into this locker, the one here on the end. But according to this key . . .

She located the other locker, the one numbered to correspond with the key. Hands shaking, she opened it, and of course, it was empty.

A voice boomed and echoed over the public address system: 'Last call for the California umtumm— the California something-or-other, departing from Gate Three is exacklum fi'min-utts. Passengers will kine-ly take their seats on the California . . .'

Five minutes!

Feverishly she returned to the first locker, fought again to unlock it. Again, as on the first occasion, the effort was futile. The drinks struggled upward again. The heat, after the air-conditioned bar, beat and pounded through her brain.

She weaved a little. Foolishly, because there was nothing else to do, she started back toward the second locker, the one the key fitted. And then she stopped dead in her tracks. Up near the entrance, hat pulled low over his eyes, Doc was watching her. Watching and then coming toward her.

A few steps away, he faced up to the locker bank, fumbling in his pocket as though seeking

99

a coin. His terse whisper whipped at her from the corner of his mouth. 'Simmer down and talk fast. What happened?'

'I – I don't know, Doc! I put the bag in that locker back there, but I've got the key to . . .'

'To another locker, one that's empty, right? What did he look like?'

'He? What do you . . .?'

'Will you in the name of all hell hurry! Someone helped you. Put the bag in for you, then switched keys on you. It's one of the oldest con gags in the country.'

'But – well, how was I to know?' she lashed out. 'You leave me to do everything . . .'

'Easy, babe, easy. I'm not blaming you.' His voice became a purring calm, the intense calm above a raging subterranean storm. 'How long since you left the bag? When you first came in, maybe an hour?'

'No. Not more than thirty minutes. But . . .'

'Good. He'd expect you to leave it longer than that. If he operates on form, he'll try to hit several times before he pulls out.' He stepped back from the lockers, jerked his head. 'Move. Go ahead of me. If you spot him, give me the office.'

'But, Doc. You shouldn't . . .'

'There's a lot of things that shouldn't have been done!' His tone was a whip again. 'Now, *move*!'

She started off at a fast walk, then broke into a faster one as his long stride kept him almost on her heels. At what was almost a trot she reached the waiting room, swept it with an anxious glance. Prodded by an urgent cough from Doc, she made a hasty survey of the adjacent areas.

Then – and now she was really trotting – she headed for the train gates. The jarring of her high heels shot fire up her ankles. A button of her blouse became undone, and she ran clutching at the gap with one hand. Frantically, she raced down the corridor, a notorious criminal on the trail of a quarter of a million stolen and restolen dollars, and somewhere within her the child she had been, the child that she was in this baffling and fearful moment, wept with sullen self-pity. It – it wasn't fair! She was tired and sick, and she didn't want to play any more. She'd never wanted to play in the first place!

And it was all so useless. The man would be gone now, no matter what Doc said. He had the money, and he'd keep it. And they, they'd have nothing. The whole nation looking for them, and no means of escape. No money but the relatively little they were carrying.

She tripped and almost fell. She caught herself, half-turned in pain and anger on Doc. And then she saw him, the thief.

He was at a row of lockers near the train gates; no more than twenty feet away from the uniformed station attendant who stood at Gate Three – *their* gate – consulting his watch. Smiling engagingly, he was opening a locker for a well-dressed elderly woman, placing two expensive cowhide bags inside.

He slammed the door, tested it. Handed her a key and picked up the money satchel. Tipping his hat, he turned away. And suddenly he saw Carol.

His expression never changed. He took a step straight toward her, smiling, apparently on the point of calling a hello. And then, with a movement that was at once abrupt and casual, he disappeared behind the lockers.

'Doc—' Carol gestured feebly.

But Doc had already spotted the satchel, identified the thief for what he was. He strode past her, and after a moment's indecision, she followed him.

By the time she had gotten behind the lockers, neither Doc nor the thief was in sight. They had disappeared as quickly and completely as though the floor had opened and swallowed them up. She turned, started to retrace her steps – and if she had, she would have seen the thief hasten through the train gate, with Doc following in brisk pursuit. Instead, however, she continued along the row of lockers, turned into the aisle formed by another row, and thence on to the end of that before coming out into the open again. By which time, of course, Doc and the thief were long since gone from view.

She stood there in the corridor, looking this way and that, seeming to shrink, to grow smaller and smaller in its lofty vastness. She had never felt so bewildered, so lost, so alone. Doc – where had he gone? How could she find him? What would happen if she couldn't?

Reason told her that he must have followed the thief onto the train. But – and here reason questioned its own statement – would a smart thief choose the train as an escape route? And would Doc have followed without a word or sign to her?

He'd have been in a hurry, of course. He would doubtless assume that she was heeling him, even as he was heeling the thief. But – suppose she was wrong. Suppose the pursuit had led back up into the station.

She wouldn't know that he wasn't on the train until she had looked, and by that time . . .

She shivered at the thought. Herself on the train, and Doc here – the two of them separated in a hostile and watchful world. He wouldn't dare to make inquiries, to look for her; even to wait around the station for her return. For that matter, he could not be sure that she hadn't taken a powder on him. After last night, that drunken hateful talk of Beynon's . . .

Maybe Doc had run out on her! Maybe he'd recovered the money and abandoned her! He was sore, she thought; more accurately, suspicious. She needed him, but he did not need her. And when Doc no longer needed a person . . .

The trainman looked at her sharply. Then, with a final glance at his watch, he slipped it into his pocket and started through the gate.

'Mister!' Carol hurried toward him. 'Did a couple of men go through here just now? A rather tall older man, and a man with a . . .'

'A couple of men?' The trainman was irritably amused. 'Lady, there's probably been a hundred. I can't . . .'

'But this was just in the last minute or so! The one in front would have had gray hair and a little mustache!'

'Were they catching the train for California?'

'I – I don't know. I mean, I think they were but . . .'

'Well, if they were, they went through here. If they weren't, they didn't.' He fidgeted impatiently with the gate. 'What about you? You taking the train?'

'I don't know!' Carol almost wailed. 'I mean, I'm not sure whether I should or not. Can't you remember . . .'

'No I can't,' he cut her off shortly. 'Kind of seems like they did, but I wouldn't say for sure.'

'But it's so important! If you'd just . . .'

'Lady—' his voice rose. 'I told you I wasn't sure whether I saw 'em or not, and that's all I can tell you, and if you're taking the train you'll have to do it right now. It's already two minutes late pulling out.'

'But . . .'

'Make up your mind, lady. What's it going to be?'

Carol looked at him helplessly. 'I guess,' she said. 'I guess I really should – shouldn't . . .'

'Yes?' he snapped. 'Well?'

Scowling, he waited a second or two more. Then, as she remained undecided, he slammed the gate and went down the ramp.

CHAPTER EIGHT

The barn was pleasantly cool – clean and sweet-smelling with the aroma of fresh straw and new hay. In one of the rear stalls a swaybacked horse nickered contentedly. From a partitioned-off kennel, also in the rear, came the happy yapping of a litter of puppies.

There were two box stalls at the front, small floored rooms open at the aisle end. Rudy Torrento was in one, propped up on a cot while the veterinarian worked over him. Opposite him, in the other, was the doctor's wife. The doc's name was Harold Clinton, so she, of course, was Mrs Clinton. Fran, her husband called her, when he wasn't addressing her sweetishly as hon or pet or lambie. But Rudy didn't think of her by any of those handles.

He's seen this babe before – her many counterparts, that is. He knew her kin, distant and near. All her mamas, sisters, aunts, cousins and what have you. And he knew the name was Lowdown with a capital L. He wasn't at all surprised to find her in a setup like this. Not after encountering her as a warden's sister-in-law, the assistant treasurer of a country bank, and a supervisor of paroles. This babe got around. She was the original square-plug-in-a-round-hole kid. But she never changed any. She had that good old Lowdown blood in her, and the right guy could bring it out.

Seated on a high stool with her bare, milk-white legs crossed and her chin cupped demurely in the palm of her hand, she watched moist-lipped as her husband completed his work. She wore an expensive-looking plaid skirt, somewhat in need of cleaning and pressing, and a tight white sweater of what appeared to be cashmere. Her shoes were scuffed, their spike heels slightly run over. But her corn-colored hair was impeccably coiffured, and her nails glistened with bright red polish.

She'd do, Rudy decided; yes, sir, little Miss Lowdown would do just fine. But that red polish would have to go, even if her eensie-teensie pinkies went right along with it.

He caught her eye, and winked at her. She frowned primly, then lowered her lashes and smoothed the sweater a degree tighter. Rudy laughed out loud.

'Feeling better, eh?' The doctor straightened, beamed down at him professionally. 'That's the glucose. Nothing like a good intravenous feeding of glucose to pull a man together fast.'

'Ain't it the truth?' Rudy grinned. 'Bet you didn't know that, did you, Mrs Clinton?'

She murmured inaudibly, then tittered that she couldn't even spell glucose. Rudy told her that her husband was a plenty smart man. 'Plenty,' he repeated. 'I've been tinkered over by high class MDs that didn't know half the medicine your old man does.'

'Well, uh, thank you.' Clinton's thin face flushed with pleasure. 'I only wish that the people around here, uh, shared your high opinion.'

'Yeah? You mean to say they don't?'

'Well . . .'

'They don't,' his wife cut in curtly. 'They think he's a dope.'

Clinton blinked at her from behind his glasses. He was either unoffended, or resigned to such offenses: doubtless the last, Rudy decided. 'Now, uh, Fran,' he said mildly, 'I don't believe I'd put it quite that way. It's just that they're rather set in their ways, and, uh, a young man like me – someone probably more interested in the theory of disease than actual practice – why . . .'

'So the sun don't rise and set here,' Rudy said. 'If the people aren't smart enough to appreciate you, why not go someplace where they are?'

'Where – where they are?' The doctor hesitated. 'I'm afraid I don't know, uh, where – how . . .'

Rudy let it lay for the moment. He asked how his condition appeared to the doctor, and Clinton replied that it was excellent. 'You have a wonderful constitution, Mr Torrento. Might even say – ha-ha – that you had the constitution of a horse.'

'Ha-ha,' said Fran Clinton. 'That's really good, Harold.'

'It's a riot,' Rudy said. 'But what about the bandages, Clint – the wound? How often should I have it looked after?'

'Well, a couple of times a day perhaps. That's barring any unusual developments.'

'How you mean, unusual?'

'Well, uh, fever. Any signs of gangrene or putrefaction. But I'm sure there won't be any. Just have it cleaned and rebandaged a couple of times a day for the next couple of days, and – and—' His voice died suddenly. He went on again, his eyes evading Rudy's. 'On second thoughts, it might be wiser if you didn't have it tended at all. Might just irritate the wound, you know. Keep it from healing.'

'It might,' Rudy nodded. 'I wouldn't know. You wouldn't maybe be kidding me would you, Clint, old boy?'

'K-kidding you? Why would I . . .'

'Because you want to get rid of me pronto, and you figure that if I need any taking care of, you'll be elected to do it.'

Rudy pulled the heavy .38 from his belt, twirled it by the trigger guard and let the butt smack into his palm. Grinning savagely, he took aim at the doctor's stomach.

'Now, maybe, you'd better have a good big third thought,' he said. 'Just think real careful and give me the truth. Will I need more lookin' after, or won't I?'

'Y-you'll – y-y-y—' It was as far as the doctor could get.

'I'll need it, huh?' Rudy flipped the gun again and shoved it back into his belt. 'Well, that's all I wanted to know. Just shoot square with me, and you got no more trouble than a flea in a dog pound. Now,' he added casually, 'I guess you want me to clear out of here.'

Clinton nodded, weakly apologetic, as he sagged down onto a canvas camp stool. 'Oh, well, you did promise, Mr Torrento. You said that . . .'

'And I'll keep my promise,' Rudy lied, 'if that's the way you want it. I'll leave, and you'll call the cops, and . . .'

'N-no! No, we won't, Mr Torrento! I . . .'

'. . . and then maybe tonight, maybe five years from now, you'd have a visitor. It'd probably be me, because I got quite a rep for breaking out of tight spots. But if I didn't make it, some pal of mine would. Anyway, you'd have a visitor – like the guy that fingered Willie Sutton had one – and you know what he'd do to you, Clint, to you and the little lady here, before he did you a big favor and killed you?'

He told them, threatened them with what would happen; lips wolfishly drawn back from his teeth; eyes holding them with an unwinking reptilian gaze. He finished the discourse, and the sudden silence was like a scream.

A drop of sweat rolled shinily down the veterinarian's nose. His wife gulped and clapped a hand to her mouth, spoke through the lattice of her fingers.

'We – he won't call any cops,' she said whitely. 'He even looks like he's going to, and I'll murder him myself!'

'Well, now, maybe he'd feel that he had to,' Rudy said. 'I'm hot as a three-dollar pistol. I need medical attention. Say I've got a three to one chance of getting away, and you're giving me the best of it. Wouldn't you figure it that way, Clint?'

Clinton cleared his throat. He opened his mouth to speak, then closed it again. Rudy beamed at him falsely.

'Kind of one of those hell-if-you-do-or-don't propositions, ain't it, Clint? You holler copper and you and Frannie get your clocks fixed. You don't do it, and you're still in the soup. They got enough on me to fry me six times. That'd bring you and Fran in on accessory raps for forty or fifty years.'

'A-accessories?' the doctor stammered. 'But how would they know that . . .'

'I'll tell them,' Rudy said cheerfully. 'I'd name you as accessories.'

'B-but – but, why? After we'd helped . . .'

'Because I'd figure you were boobs,' Rudy said, 'and boobs I got a very low boiling point for.'

Clinton shook his head in bewilderment. Helplessly, hopefully, he looked at his wife. There was some indefinable change in her expression, something that carried a chill shock and yet

110

seemed entirely natural to her. He had a feeling that he had never seen her before; that she was at once a stranger to him and an old friend of Torrento's.

'What,' she said, 'is the proposition – Rudy?'

'What do you think? That you and Clinty boy go along with me.'

'And?'

'I fork up for a new car. I pay all expenses, and me, I wouldn't kick on a little expense like a mink jacket. You get anything you want, as soon as we're where we're safe to buy it. You cross the country first-class, and when we hit California there'll be a ten-grand bonus.'

Her eyes gleamed softly. 'That sounds good,' she murmured. 'That sounds real good, Rudy.'

'Good, hell,' Rudy said. 'It's perfect. Big dough for you, a new car, and a swell trip. And not a chance in the world of getting caught. Clint bandages me up so that no one can see what I look like – I been in a bad accident, see? Then . . .'

'I won't do it.' Clinton had found his voice at last. 'We are not going with you, Mr Torrento.'

'You shut up!' His wife glared at him fiercely. 'I guess I've got something to say about what we're going to do!'

'Now, take it easy,' Rudy said. 'What's wrong with the deal, Clint? I thought it added up good for you, but maybe I could sweeten it a little.'

'What's wrong with it?' The doctor waved his hands wildly. 'Why – why, everything's wrong! I'm a respected citizen, a professional man. I can't just throw everything I am overboard, and go gallivanting across the country with a – uh – I couldn't do it for any amount of money!'

'Why couldn't you?' Rudy asked interestedly.

'Well – uh – because! I just got through telling you!'

'The respected citizen gimmick? But you ain't going to be one, remember? You won't be very long, anyway, unless you figure on being a dead one with a hide full of broken bones and a pound of raw hamburger for a face.'

'He's already dead,' his wife snapped contemptuously. Then, her manner changing, she slid off the stool, crossed the aisle and knelt at Clinton's side. 'Now, Harold, hon,' she coaxed, 'why do you want to act like this? Don't you love me any more? Don't you want me to be happy? We could have such a wonderful life together, hon. Not having to worry and fret about money all the time, and people respecting and looking up to you, instead of laughing and joking like . . .'

'But, Fran!' The doctor squirmed. 'I – you know I love you and want you to be happy, but . . .'

'That's been your whole trouble, hon. Money. You just didn't have the money to get started off right. Oh, I know how smart and wonderful my lambie is, even if I haven't always acted like it, and I could just absolutely cry some-

112

times when I think how different it could be for him. Just think of it, lambie! Starting out in a new place, with everything we need to make a good impression. Good clothes, and a swell car and a decent place to live. And a real office for you, hon. A nice big office, and a fine big laboratory where you could carry on your experiments . . .'

She held him close, and over his shoulder she winked at Rudy. Clinton twitched and sputtered, simultaneously attempting – it seemed – to return her embrace and disengage himself from it. His protests grew weaker and fewer. Finally, as a last resort, he professed a willingness to take on the enterprise, he *wanted* to do it. But the potential danger made it unthinkable.

'We might have an accident, and they'd find out who Mr Torrento was. Or the police might just stop us on suspicion – you know, one of those routine investigations. A lot of criminals get caught that way and . . .'

'A lot of people get nibbled to death by wild ducks,' Rudy yawned. 'But I'll tell you what I'll do, Clint. We get a bad break like you mention, and you and Fran can be hostages. I'll back you up on it. You're helping me because I'd've killed you if you hadn't.'

Clinton sighed, and gave up. All his life he had given up. He didn't know why it was like that; why a man who wanted nothing but to live honestly and industriously and usefully – who, briefly, asked only the privileges of giving

113

and helping – had had to compromise and surrender at every turn. But that was the way it had been, and that apparently was the way it was to be.

'I suppose it doesn't seem to you that I'm giving up much, Mr Torrento,' he said dully. 'But to me—' he paused, his eyes straying to the swaybacked mare, and his voice gathered new strength. 'They're awfully smart, Mr Torrento. You wouldn't believe how smart and, uh, nice they can be. Why, you take something like a pig or even a garter snake, and pet it and feed it and fix up whatever's wrong with it – just treat it like you'd want to be treated if you were what it is . . .'

'Oh, put it in a book.' His wife jumped to her feet. 'We've got things to do.'

Rudy's car was driven into the weed-choked and rocky pasture, buried beneath a stack of moldering hay. (It is still there if anyone cares to look.) The doctor's business and professional affairs were wound up by two brief telephone calls, ending his lease and turning over his practice to another veterinarian. Neither the landlord nor the other vet was surprised by this action, or its nominal abruptness. Clinton had been barely eking out an existence. The run-down acres and the tumbledown house, rented furnished, had discouraged far more resourceful and tenacious tenants than he.

After taking Rudy's temperature again and urging him to rest, Clinton drove away in his ancient jalopy. He had more than three thousand dollars of Rudy's money in his wallet. His destination was a nearby city, where the cash purchase of a car would arouse no suspicion.

Fran Clinton waved him a loving good-bye from the doorway of the barn, then sauntered back, hips swinging, and resumed her stool opposite Rudy. 'Well,' she smirked, 'how'd you like the way I handled stupid?'

'The doc, you mean?' Rudy crooked a finger at her. 'Come here.'

'What for?'

Rudy stared at her steadily, not answering. The knowing smile on her face wavered a little, but she slid off the stool and came across the aisle. She started to step up into the stall where Rudy lay. Without the slightest change of expression, he kicked her in the stomach; watched unwinking, as she landed floundering and groaning in the straw of the aisle.

She staggered to her feet, gasping, eyes tear-washed with anger and pain. She asked furiously just what was the big idea anyway? Just who the hell did he think he was anyway? Then, weakly, as he continued to stare at her in silence, she began to weep.

'I d-didn't do anything. I – I tried to be n-nice, and do what you wanted me to, and y-you . . .'

She was overwhelmed with self-pity. Blindly, as though drawn by a magnet, she came close to Rudy again. And he hooked her, stumbling, into the stall with his foot, brought her down on her knees with a yank of a viselike hand. The hand went to the back of her head. Her mouth crushed cruelly against his. She gasped and struggled for a moment; then, with a greedy moan, she surrendered, squirming and pressing her softness against him.

Abruptly, Rudy pushed her away. 'You get the idea?' he said. 'When I tell you to do something, you do it. Fast! Think you can remember that?'

'Oh, yes,' she said, eyes glowing softly. 'Anything you say, Rudy. You just tell me and – and whatever it is – I'll . . .'

He told her what she was to do. Then, as she looked at him, face falling, he pointed up the command with a twist of her arm. 'Now, hop to it,' he said. 'Get that red paint off your claws. It's making me sick.'

CHAPTER NINE

Doc followed the thief through the gate to the train, then down the winding ramp to the loading platform. The man was nowhere in sight when he emerged from the tunnel. But Doc had not expected him to be. Stepping behind a nearby pillar, he waited watchfully. And after a minute or two the thief edged out from behind another pillar and started back up the platform.

Doc confronted him abruptly. 'All right, mister,' he said. 'I'll just – ' His hand grasped for the bag, almost gripped the handle. The thief twisted it, yanked, and trotted back down the platform. Doc strode after him.

He had made a mistake, he knew. Back there in the station he should have shouted at the thief, shouted that he *was* a thief. In which case the man would certainly have dropped the bag and fled. But he had been afraid to call out, had even believed that it wouldn't be necessary. Caught red-handed, the thief would – or should – hightail it.

Unfortunately, the man was as unobliging as

he was discerning. He had stolen this tall gent's bag, or his wife's bag. The wife had been nervous as all hell about it, and now this guy, her husband, was making no outcry at all. That must be because he couldn't.

So the thief made off, taking the bag with him. More than a little hopeful that Doc would not risk pursuing him. As much exultant as dismayed when he saw that Doc was right after him. This must be something big that he had latched onto. And with Doc unable to squawk, he stood a good chance of getting away with it. Or at least a part of it. He could demand a split of whatever the bag contained.

The thief was very cocksure, it should be said; in his particular branch of crime, he had to be. Also – and it is hardly necessary to point this out – he had known no criminals of Doc McCoy's caliber.

Only two doors of the train were open, one in the Pullman section, the other to admit coach passengers. The thief approached the latter squeezing himself in line behind an elderly couple. The conductor stopped them as they started to climb aboard.

'Tickets, tickets, please,' he intoned impatiently. 'See your ticket, lady, mister.'

It developed that the tickets were at the bottom of the lady's handbag. While she fumbled for them anxiously, the thief eased around her and got a foot on the steps.

'Ticket? Ticket, mister?' the conductor called to him.

But the thief was already in the car.

The conductor glowered. The elderly woman produced one of the two necessary tickets, then, pawing for the other, she spilled a handful of small change onto the platform. Immediately she and her husband stopped to gather it up. The conductor implored them to please step aside, folks. 'Tickets, tickets. Kindly show your tickets.' But he himself was pushed aside as the other passengers pressed forward, began to clamber aboard by the twos and threes. And what with one thing and another, he not only was unable to check their tickets but he ceased to give a damn whether he did.

With a heavenward gesture, he stalked away to converse with a sympathetically grinning brakeman.

Meanwhile, Doc was on the train, trailing the thief by less than a car length.

The man had turned right, heading toward the front of the train. He moved with relatively little haste as long as he was within Doc's view. But losing him momentarily in passing from one car to another, he began to run. His intent or, rather, hope was to get off the train and leave Doc to it. But that would take time, as his hurried attempt to open a connecting door proved. He would need at least a couple of minutes to jump off and lose himself and so he ran.

The passengers became fewer and fewer as he neared the front of the train. He raced through one in which there were none at all; and then, coming to the door at its end, he stopped short. The car ahead was a dingy, straw-seated smoker. It was wholly empty, like the one he was in, and it adjoined the first of the express cars. In other words, he could go no farther. And he still lacked the time, or was afraid that he did, to make his escape.

His thief's mind weighed the situation, made an almost instantaneous decision. Darting through the drapes of the men's rest room, he yanked down the window shade, tossed the bag onto the leather couch and pressed the catches which held it shut. He was going to get *something* out of this frammis. Make sure, at least, that there was something to get. After all, the world was full of screwballs and it just might be that there was nothing in this keister but old matchbook covers or . . .

He gasped when he saw what was in it. Automatically, he grabbed a thick packet of bills and shoved them into his inside coat pocket. Then, hearing an approaching telltale sound, he slammed the bag shut, pushed it under the couch, and flattened himself against the wall by the doorway.

The train jerked and began to move. Doc's swift footsteps came closer. Then the drapes rustled, and in the mirror above the lavatory the thief saw his pursuer glance inside.

There was a muttered curse of disappointment. Then the drapes fell back into place, and the car door wheezed open and shut. The thief stayed where he was, motionless, hardly breathing. Some thirty seconds passed. The train slowly gathered speed. It still wasn't going too fast for a man to jump off, but . . .

There was a muted clang. The grating and scraping of metal against metal. Then silence save for the clicking of the wheels. Exultantly, the thief let out his breath.

He pulled the bag from beneath the couch and stepped out into the vestibule. The metal platform above the steps was swinging free, and the lower half of the exit door was partly open. The thief laughed out loud. What a break! Boy, what a break! Him speeding toward California with a satchelful of dough, and the guy back there at the station looking for him. And he couldn't raise a beef about his loss!

Grinning, he reclosed and locked the exit door. He entered the next car, the smoker, threw two seats together and tossed the bag onto the overhead rack. He sat down, placing his feet comfortably on the seat ahead of him.

And Doc moved away from the rear wall of the car, and sat down at his side. The thief gaped; his stiff lips framed a silent question. Doc jerked his head over his shoulder. 'Back there,' he said. 'In the same place you were, approximately, when you hid in the rest room. I'll tell you something,' he added. 'Whenever you can see someone in a mirror, you can also be seen.'

'B-but—' the thief shook his head helplessly. 'But . . .'

'I wanted to get you out of the rest room, and it wouldn't have looked well to carry you – just in case someone was looking. And of course you'd head this way instead of going back the way you came.' He smiled unpleasantly, prodding the thief's ribs with his gun. 'That's the mark of a punk, you know. He loves a cinch. I'd jumped the train, supposedly, and it was traveling fast. But you were still too gutless to go back into the cars. You were afraid I might spot you from the platform and hop back on.'

He was very annoyed with the thief. The man had given him an extremely bad time, and he was apt to receive an even worse one from Carol as an aftermath. He had seen her just before he sat down, motioned to her as she hesitantly entered the car behind. And while he couldn't tell much about her expression at that distance, he could see that she was angry. He had known that she must be before she showed up; as soon as, having cornered the thief, he had had time to think of anything else.

'Put the rod away, mister.' The thief was smiling, getting back his nerve. 'You aren't going to use it.'

'That's another mark of a punk,' Doc told him. 'He doesn't know when to be frightened.'

'You can't use it. You can't make any kind of rumble. If you could, you'd've already done it.' He winked at Doc companionably. 'We're two of a kind, mister. You . . .'

'Now that,' Doc said, 'is carrying things too far.'

And he whipped the gun barrel upward.

It smashed against the point of the thief's chin. His eyes glazed, and his body went into a sacklike sag. Methodically, Doc locked an arm around his head, braced the other across his back and jerked.

It was over in a split second. If a man can die instantly, the thief did.

Doc tilted the back a little, adjusted the man's body to a slight reclining position. He placed his feet on the seat ahead, and pulled his hat over his eyes.

Doc studied the corpse critically. He gave it a few minor touches – closing the staring eyes, putting one of the limp hands into a coat pocket – and was satisfied. To all appearances the man was asleep. Even Carol thought he was – or would have, if she had not known otherwise.

She sat down facing Doc, her anger somewhat weakened by the relief at being reunited with him. He hadn't had it very easy either, she guessed. And the terrifying mixup at the station was probably more her own fault than his. Still . . .

She couldn't quite locate the cause of her anger; explain, in absolute terms, why she had viewed him and almost everything he had done with distrust and distaste practically from the moment of their post-robbery meeting. It wasn't so much what he'd done, she supposed, as what he had not. Not so much what he was, as what he was not. And in her mind she wailed bridelike for what she had lost – or thought she had; for something that had never existed outside of her mind.

He doesn't treat me like he used to, she thought. He's not the same man any more.

'Carol –' Doc spoke to her a second time. 'I said I was sorry, dear.'

She looked at him coldy, shrugged. 'All right. What's the pitch now?'

'That depends. Has the conductor collected your ticket – no? Well, that's good. But he did see you when you got on?'

Carol shook her head. 'The train was already moving. If the porter hadn't hopped off and helped me – well, never mind. The less said about that the better.'

'Perhaps. For the moment at least.' Doc looked back through the door, saw the conductor trudging up the aisle of the next car. 'Now give me one of the tickets – for my friend here – and just follow my lead.'

The conductor was grumbling, complaining, almost before he reached them. What was the sense in their coming way up here? It was uncomfortable for them, and it made things hard on him. Doc murmured apologies. Their friend had wanted to visit the diner; having come this far in the wrong direction, he had decided to remain.

'My wife and I are getting off at the first stop,' he added, proferring a bill along with the ticket. 'We hadn't planned to . . .'

'You're getting off?' the conductor exploded. 'This isn't some commuter's local, mister. You shouldn't have got on without a ticket; shouldn't've stayed on any way.'

'And we hadn't planned to. But this gentleman wasn't feeling well and . . .'

'Then he shouldn't have got on either! Or he ought to've bought himself some Pullman space.' He jabbed a train check into the window clip, yanked a coupon from the ticket book and tossed it down onto the seat. 'You don't have enough money there, mister,' he snapped at Doc. 'The first scheduled stop for this train is ten o'clock tonight.'

Carol's mouth tightened nervously. Ten o'clock – more than nine hours from now! They could never maintain the masquerade of the 'sleeping' man that long. The conductor was already studying him narrow-eyed, turning a suspicious gaze toward Doc.

'What's the matter with him anyway?' he said. 'He acts like he was drunk or doped or something. Here, you,' he started to grab the corpse by the shoulder. 'What . . .'

Doc caught his hand, grimly rose up from the seat. 'I'll tell you what's the matter with him,' he said. 'He got a bad jostling when he boarded the train. Started up an old neck injury. You didn't notice because you were off chatting with a friend instead of minding your job. But I've got several witnesses to the fact that it happened, and if you're looking for trouble I'll be glad to supply it.'

The conductor's mouth opened and reopened.

125

He swallowed heavily. Doc softened his tone, warmed him with a look of man-to-man sympathy.

'Now, I know a man can't be everyplace at once,' he said. 'I don't always follow rules right to the letter, and I don't expect anyone else to. And as long as my friend isn't seriously injured, we're both inclined to forget the matter. On the other hand . . . '

He let the words hang in the air. The conductor glanced at his watch, took out a receipt book. 'Suppose we pull a stop for you in about an hour? I could do it sooner, I guess, but we might get a flag there anyway, and . . .'

'An hour? That will be fine,' Doc said.

'And, uh, everything'll be okay with your friend? I mean, you don't think he'll, uh . . .'

'File a complaint? Don't give it a thought,' Doc said heartily. 'I'll guarantee that he won't.'

He sat down again as the conductor left, and tucked the railroad ticket into the breast pocket of the dead man's coat. Carol watched him, a little misty-eyed, feeling a sudden resurgence of the slavish devotion and adoration which had been about to be lost to the past.

Everything had been such a mess. Everything had seemed so different – she, Doc – everything. But now the mess was gone, the mistakes and misunderstandings brushed away – or aside. And Doc was exactly the same Doc she had dreamed of and longed for these last four years.

Relief engulfed her. Relief and gratitude at being snatched back from a last-straw, not-to-be-

126

borne peril. She had been sinking, coming apart inside, and Doc had saved her and made her whole again. Impulsively she reached out and squeezed his hand.

'Doc,' she said. 'Do me a favor?'

'Practically anything.' Doc said instantly into her mood.

'If I ever get nasty again, give me a good hard kick in the pants.'

Doc said he would have to investigate the possibility of breakage first; he had a very delicate foot. Then he laughed and she laughed. And quivering with the movement of the train, the dead man seemed to laugh too.

When they got off the train, Doc waved a smiling good-bye toward the window, then advised the conductor that his friend was doing nicely. 'I gave him some aspirin and he's going back to sleep for a while. That's all he needs, just rest and quiet.'

The conductor said there was no reason at all why the gentleman shouldn't get it. 'He can sleep till Doomsday as far as I'm concerned!'

Doc thanked him for his courtesy and gave him a warm handshake. As the train pulled out, the conductor examined the bill he had received during the handshaking process. And glowing pleasantly – telling himself you could always spot a gentleman – he started back down the line of cars. His happy musings were interrupted with nerve-shattering suddenness by a screamed demand to 'Stick 'em up!'

The owner of the voice had been crouching between two seats. He was about seven, dressed in cowboy regalia, and equipped anachronistically with a toy machine gun.

'What are you doing here?' the conductor gasped, his hair slowly setting back to his scalp. 'I've told you about fifteen times already to stay with your moth . . .'

'Bang, bang, bang!' The boy screamed. 'You're an old stinky booger man, an' I'm gonna shoot you dead!'

He dropped into a crouch, triggered the gun. It chattered and barked realistically. Even more realistic was the water which jetted from its muzzle, and sprayed the conductor's starched white shirt-front. The conductor grabbed at him. The boy fled, screaming with laughter, shrieking insults and threats, spreading consternation through the next six cars until he reached the sanctuary of his mother. She responded to his pursuer's complaints with a kind of arch crossness.

'Oh, my goodness! Such a fuss over one little boy. Do you expect him to just sit still with his hands folded?'

She glanced around, smiling, at the other passengers, soliciting approval. None was forthcoming. The conductor said that he expected her to keep an eye on her son; to see that he cease his rambunctious ramblings forthwith.

'I mean that, lady. I'm insisting on it. I don't want to find that young man outside of this car again.'

'But I just don't *understand*!' The woman frowned prettily. 'What possible *difference* does it make if the poor child moves around a little? He's not hurting anything.'

'But he might get hurt. In fact,' the conductor added grimly, 'he's very likely to. And you'd be the first to complain if he did.'

He trudged away, reflecting that it was such brats and such mothers who provided unanswerable argument for the proponents of capital punishment. *Bang, bang, bang!* he brooded bitterly. *Ol' stinky booger man.* I'd like to boogerman him!

If he could have looked ahead a few hours – but he could not, fortunately. It would have been much to bear, in his mood, to see the boy acclaimed, however briefly, as brave, bold, brilliant and, in sum, a national hero.

Which is just what happened.

Doc McCoy had a fairly good map of the United States in his mind, surprisingly detailed, and as up-to-date as he could keep it. So, leaving the train, he inquired about a remembered landmark – although it was ten years since he had been in the area. And learning that it was still in existence, he and Carol taxied out to the place.

It was some five miles out on the highway, a family-style roadhouse set down amidst several acres of picnic grounds. They had lunch inside the establishment; then, taking several bottles of beer with them, they located a secluded picnic table and settled down for the brief wait until nightfall.

They could not get a car before then; at any rate, it would not be wise to attempt it. And the way they intended to get it made night travel advisable. A hot car was always cooler at night – providing, of course, that its loss was unreported. People weren't so alert. There was a sharp reduction in the risk of raising some yokel who knew the owner.

'And there's no big hurry,' Doc pointed out. 'I've got a hunch that our late traveling companion will go right on sleeping, undisturbed, until that ten o'clock stop. Even if they found out the nature of his slumber before then, it wouldn't matter much. The body has to be posted. That takes time, and it can't be done in just any hick village. Then there's the conductor's story of an old neck injury – along with the conductor's guilty conscience – to add confusion to the proceedings.' He laughed softly. 'If I know anything about human nature, he'll swear that our friend was alive and in good health at the time we left him.'

Carol nodded, laughing with him. This was the old Doc talking, her Doc. She wanted more of his warming reassurance, and Doc did his best to supply it.

'Of course, we will be suspected of bringing about the gentleman's death,' he went on. 'Sometime tomorrow, say, when the conductor has come clean and it's definitely determined that the broken neck was inflicted rather than accidental. But who are we, anyway? What good is our description if they don't have a channel for it? Now, if there was anything to indicate we were bank robbers, we'd be tabbed in five minutes. Just as quickly as a batch of "wanted" cards could be run through the sorter.'

'It's not going to happen,' Carol said firmly. 'So let's not talk about it.'

'Right,' Doc said. 'No point to it at all.'

'But it's still smart to get off the highway. One more night is as much as we can risk.'

'Well, that may be putting it a little strong. We won't be tagged with Beynon's car, and we helped our chances with that long jump north. Let's just say that the railroad still seems like our best bet.'

Obviously, he continued, they couldn't go back to the line they'd been on. In fact, any of the due-west routes were a poor risk; unless – and the time element precluded this – they were able to take one across the northern rim of the United States.

'So I'd say we do this. Pull another swingback; get completely away from this east-west travel route. We can push hard tonight, make Tulsa or Oklahoma City by morning, and take a southern route train. We can miss Los Angeles that way. Come into California through the Carisso Gorge, and then straight on into San Diego. We can make it in forty-eight hours if everything goes all right.'

'And it will, Doc.' Carol squeezed his hand. 'I know it!'

'Of course it will,' Doc said.

Actually, he was more than a little uneasy about the situation. There was much that he disliked about it. But since it could not be changed, he put the best possible face on it, if he was secretly, perhaps subconsciously, annoyed at the necessity for doing so.

Much of their predicament was Carol's fault. She should have been absolutely frank with him about Beynon. Failing that – having made that one serious error – she should have kept the bag with her at the Kansas City station. That was little enough to expect of her, wasn't it? It was simple enough. But she had had to blunder again, again forcing him to plan extemporaneously, which was another way of saying dangerously. And now, instead of being properly apologetic, willing to look the facts in the face, she had to be cajoled and bolstered up.

If I'd known she was going to be like this, he thought – and left the thought at that. He took another drink of the beer, smiling at her, inwardly grinning the wry, pained grin of a man who has bumped his elbow.

'Doc.' She was looking down at the table, idly scratching at the chipped paint with a fingernail. 'Doc,' she raised her eyes. 'I've changed a lot, haven't I? You think I have.'

'Oh, well,' Doc began. 'After all, it's been . . .'

'You seem the same way to me, Doc. Almost

like a stranger at times. I mean – well, I don't mean it as though I was criticizing or blaming you or anything, I've seemed to have done something dopey every time I turned around, and you've been a damn sight nicer about it than you should have been. But . . .'

'Now, don't feel that way.' Doc laid a hand over hers. 'We've had some bad luck. We've never been involved in anything quite like this before.'

'I don't think that's the trouble. Not the real trouble. We had our difficulties before, and they didn't seem to matter. We were so much closer, and –' she hesitated, thoughtfully. 'I guess that's it, isn't it? We kind of are strangers. We aren't the same people we were four years ago.'

'Essentially the same,' Doc disagreed. 'Let's say that perhaps we've forgotten what those people were like. In toto, I mean. We've forgotten their bad times, the occasions when they rubbed each other the wrong way, and remembered only the good.'

'Well – maybe. Yes,' she added. 'I suppose that is it.'

'I know it is. Just as soon as we've gotten a little reacquainted – have time for something besides running . . .'

'Doc.' She looked down at the table again, a faint blush spreading over her cheeks. 'I think we should, you know, get really acquainted again. I think we've just about got to. Very soon. C-can't we – isn't there some way we could manage to – be together?'

Doc murmured that he was sure they could. Beneath the table, he pressed her ankle with his, and the silken flesh quivered in response.

He began to feel a lot better about her, about everything. His inherent optimism reasserted itself, smothering his worries, recreating him in the delightful and irresistible image that had burned so bright in Carol's memory.

'I know we can't lay over, stop anywhere,' she said. 'But, well, do you suppose we could travel together on the train? Take a stateroom or a bedroom, and . . .'

Doc said he thought so; he was pretty sure of it (although he wasn't sure). 'We'll count on it, anyway. *I'll* count on it, my dear.'

And Carol blushed and squirmed deliciously.

In the deceptive half-light of dusk, Doc walked down the highway a couple of hundred yards and took cover behind a hedgerow. Carol, meanwhile, took up a position at the edge of the picnic grounds – protected by the thickening shadows of the driveway but within a quick step of the road.

Doc heard two cars stop for her, then speed on again almost before they had stopped. Soon there was a third car, and the opening and slamming of a door. And Doc came out of his place of concealment.

The car stopped for him jerkily; Carol was holding a gun in the driver's ribs. Doc climbed into the back seat and, putting a gun to the man's head, ordered him to relinquish the wheel. The man did so, fearfully, too frightened for speech, limbs stiff and numb as he slid over in the seat. With Carol driving, they moved on again.

Naturally, the car was from out-of-state; had it borne local license plates, Carol would never had gotten into it. The owner was a salesman, a man of about thirty-five with a plump well-fed face and a wide good-natured mouth. Doc spoke to him soothingly, putting him as much at ease as the circumstances would allow.

'We're sorry to do this,' he apologized. 'Believe me, we've never done anything like it before. But we ran out of money, and the wife can't take another night on the road, so – I hope you understand. You're a married man yourself, I take it.'

The salesman wasn't. He'd tried the double harness once and it hadn't worked.

'Oh, that's too bad,' Doc murmured. 'Now, I wonder if you could drive us down into Oklahoma? I can get some money there, and . . .'

'S-sure, I could! Glad to!' The salesman was pitiful in his eagerness. 'Naw, I really mean it. I was figuring on taking a fling at Tulsa myself, just for kicks, y'know. I'm not due back in Chicago for three days yet, but I already made all my calls and . . .'

Doc slugged him with the gun barrel. The man grunted, and slumped foward. Carol gave him a shove, pushed him down on the floor of the car.

'Side road, Doc?' She spoke over her shoulder.

*   *   *

Back on the train, the boy in the cowboy suit napped, dined and resumed his wanderings. After a longer absence than usual, he returned to his mother, shouting brassily that he had just killed a robber man. 'I did so, too!' he screamed, as she laughed, indulgently. 'I told him to stick 'em up an' he didn't so I poked him an' he fell over dead, an' the money he stole fell out of his pocket an' I got it! I got it right here!' He pulled a thick sheaf of bills from his blouse, waved them about excitedly. Across the aisle a man reached out and took it from him; frowned, startled, as he read the imprint on the paper banding. The Bank of Beacon City! Why, that was the place that had been robbed yesterday morning! He jumped up and went in search of the conductor.

Doc frisked the salesman, taking his wallet and all other identification. Then, with the whispering of the car's radio fading behind him, he dragged the man down the ditch to the culvert and placed the gun muzzle inside his mouth. He triggered the gun twice. He shoved it back into his belt, began squeezing the now faceless body into the culvert.

'Doc!' Carol's voice came to him urgently. 'Doc!'

'Be right with you,' he called back easily. 'Just as soon as I . . .'

The car's starter whirred. The motor coughed, caught and roared. Doc hastily clambered up the side of the ditch, yanked open the door and climbed in.

'What's the matter?' he demanded. 'Can't I leave you for two minutes without . . .'

Then he broke off, listened incredulously to the newscaster's staccato voice:

'. . . The man has been positively identified as Doc (Carter) McCoy, notorious bank robber and criminal mastermind. Police are certain that the woman with him is his wife, Carol. Their descriptions follow . . .'

CHAPTER TEN

Rudy Torrento and the Clintons started for California the morning after his arrival at their place. He was running a slight temperature, feeling worse than he had the day before. And Clinton suggested anxiously that they take it very easy for a day or so. But Rudy, fearful that Doc and Carol might get away from him, wouldn't hear of it. They were going to make California in three days, see? Three days and nights of steady driving. He himself would take a turn at the wheel if he had to, and if he *did* have to, they'd wish that he hadn't.

Then, late that evening, he heard the news about Doc and Carol; knew immediately that there was no longer any need for hurry. For certainly they would not be able to. The way things looked to him, he could probably roller-skate his way to California – and Golie's tourist court – and get there ahead of them.

So he informed the Clintons amiably that he had changed his mind. He'd decided to take Clinty-boy's advice after all, because what the hell was the use of having a doctor if you didn't listen to him? Anyway, they'd take it easy like Clint said, just take their time and get a little fun out of the trip; and they'd start in right now by turning in at a good motel.

They took connecting cabins, but only for the sake of appearances. They used only one of them, the three of them sleeping crosswise and partly disrobed in one bed, with Fran Clinton in the middle.

'Now we won't be getting lost from each other,' Rudy explained, grinning. 'Clint won't have to worry about me sneakin' off to the police, and reporting him for practicing medicine without a license.'

Mrs Clinton smirked lewdly. Rudy winked at her husband. 'It's okay with you, ain't it, Clint? You've got no objections?'

'Why, no. No, of course not,' Clinton said hastily. 'It's, uh, very sensible.' And he winced as his wife laughed openly.

He did not know how to object. In his inherent delicacy and decency, he could not admit that there was anything to object to. He heard them that night – and subsequent nights of their leisurely journey westward. But he kept his back turned and his eyes closed, feeling no shame or anger but only an increasing sickness of soul.

Just inside the border of California, while Rudy dozed in the car and Fran Clinton thumbed through a movie magazine, her husband wandered off among the trees.

He did not return. When they found him, he was lying face down in a pool of blood, one of his small hands still gripping the razor blade with which he had cut his throat.

Rudy dropped down to the ground at his side. Clutching himself, he began to rock back and forth, groaning and gasping with what Mrs Clinton mistook for a paroxysm of laughter. She could hardly be blamed for her error. She had never seen Rudy grief-stricken; the Piehead, overwhelmed by sorrow or laughter, appeared much the same.

So she began to laugh – with him, she thought. And Rudy came abruptly out of his fit and slugged her in the stomach. He beat her black and blue; everywhere but in her face. Except that he needed her, he would have beaten her to death. Then he made her carry the body into the bushes and cover it over with rocks.

She never again gave him any reason to beat her. On the contrary, no one could have been more worshipful or watchful of his whims. Yet hardly a day passed after their arrival at Golie's that he did not pound and pummel her at least once. Because she annoyed him with her groveling. Because he was restless. Because he was very worried about Doc.

'Come on, boy,' he would mumble fiercely, sitting hunched in front of the radio. 'You can do it, Doc! You done it before, an' you can do it again!'

He seldom mentioned Carol in these injunctions; seldom thought of her. She would be with Doc, and as long as he was safe, so was she. Rudy couldn't see them as splitting up, getting fed up to the point of wanting to split. Like 'em or not, those two were really nuts about each other. And Rudy was sure that nothing short of prison or death could break them up. Just in case, though . . .

Rudy grinned evilly, considering the impossible possibility of a falling out between Carol and Doc. It couldn't happen, but if it did, it wouldn't change a thing.

Carol needed Doc; she'd never been on the run before, and she'd never make it without him. And because she wouldn't, Doc couldn't split with her or let her split with him. She'd be too apt to rattle the cup on him. Buy herself a deal at his expense.

They were tied together, bound together inextricably. And Rudy roared with crazy laughter when he thought what would happen if either attempted any untying. That would be something to see, one of them trying to get the jump on the other. Hell, it would be like trying to do something with your right hand without letting the left know about it.

They were still very hot news. Rudy himself was mentioned frequently but the focus was mainly on Carol and Doc.

They'd been seen in New York, Florida, and New Orleans. They'd boarded a train for Canada, a plane for South America, a ship for the Straits Settlements. It was mostly nut stuff, Rudy guessed, the kind of hooroosh that always sprang up around a big name or a big kill. But not all of it.

Doc had friends everywhere. The really slick rumor-planting – the stuff that got more than a second look from the cops – would be their work, done to repay an old favor or simply to give a hand to a brother in need. One of their stunts even had Rudy going for a while.

Two stiffs were found in a burned-down house in Washington DC. They were charred beyond recognition, but of a size with Carol and Doc, and the women's almost melted ring bore the inscription *D to C*. As a clinching bit of evidence, the fire-blackened refrigerator was found to contain several packets of small bills, all banded with Bank of Beacon City tape.

The police were sure they had found the remains of Carol and Doc. So, almost, was Rudy. Then some eager beaver of a lab hound had managed to raise a latent print on the man's corpse, establishing him indisputably as an underworld in-and-outer who had acquired a bad name for reliability. And with this much to go on, the police hunted out the printing shop where the bank bands had been obtained. Aside from admitting that they had been made from his stock and type, the owner denied all knowledge of them. He was of the opinion, however, that the bank had been turned out during a burglary of his shop – said burglary having been duly reported to the police several days before.

So the hoax was exposed, if not the hoaxers.

No one seemed interested in learning their identity. No one seemed to care who the woman had been. Rudy wondered about her in his weirdly oblique way, and was sullenly envious of Doc. The in-and-outer had been a bum, a no-good with neither the physical attractiveness nor the cash to attract a lady friend. So, apparently, Doc's friends had arbitrarily provided him with one. Just any dame that met certain specifications. They weren't sore at her, as they were with the man. It was a hundred to one that they didn't even know her. They'd snatched her and bumped her simply to help Doc.

Rudy was forced to admit that he had no such good friends. Even little Max Vonderscheid would never kill anyone to help him. Not that he cared; if a double-crosser like Doc had friends, then he could do without 'em. But just the same . . .

'Come on, Doc,' he pleaded. 'Come to Rudy, Doc. What the hell's holding you up anyway?'

CHAPTER ELEVEN

Flight is many things. Something clean and swift, like a bird skimming across the sky. Or something filthy and crawling; a series of crab-like movements through figurative and literal slime, a process of creeping ahead, jumping sideways, running backward.

It is sleeping in fields and river bottoms. It is bellying for miles along an irrigation ditch. It is back roads, spur railroad lines, the tailgate of a wildcat truck, a stolen car and a dead couple in lovers' lane. It is food pilfered from freight cars, garments taken from clotheslines; robbery and murder, sweat and blood. The complex made simple by the alchemy of necessity.

You cannot do what you must unaided. So throughout your struggling, your creeping and running, your thieving and killing, you are on the hunt for help. And if you live, you find it, sooner or later. Rudy Torrento found his sooner, in the Clintons. Doc found his later in a family of migratory farm workers; share-croppers turned crop tramps.

There were nine of them, husband and wife and seven stair-step children – the youngest a toddling tot, the eldest a rawboned boy who was the scantling shadow of his father. They were camped alongside the muddy trickle of a creek. Two of the tires on their ancient truck were flat, and its battery stood on the ground. Their clothes were ragged but clean. When Doc emerged from the underbrush and approached them, trailed nervously by Carol, they drew together in a kind of phalanx; and the same look of wary phlegmatism was on every one of their sun-tanned faces.

Carol had no reason to be nervous. Doc knew people; and having been born among them, he knew this kind very well. Their existence was centred around existing. They had no hope of anything more, no comprehension that there might be anything more. In a sense they were an autonomous body, functioning within a society which was organized to grind them down. The law did not protect them; for them it was merely an instrument of harassment, a means of moving them on when it was against their interest to move, or detaining them where it was to their disadvantage to stay.

Doc knew them well. He knew how to talk to them.

Beyond a casual nod, he ignored the man's wife and brood. They had no authority, and to imply any to them would have been discourteous. Dragging the man aside, he spoke to him circuitously; casually hunkering down on his heels, talking with the man's own languid caution. Sometimes whole minutes passed in silence. And speaking, they seemed to discuss almost everything but the subject at hand.

Yet they understood each other, and they came to an agreement quite quickly. Doc gave the man some bills, not many and none of them large. For integrity cannot be bought, and they were simply men in need assisting one another. Then the man gave drawled instructions to his family.

'These here folks is friends,' he said. 'They'll be movin' on with us. We don't let on about it to no one, not any peep or whistle.'

He sent the eldest boy and the second eldest into town for 'new' secondhand tires, a battery and food. In the morning they headed westward, and lying prone in the rear of the truck, Doc and Carol heard the woman's cracked voice raised in a spiritual and they smelled the smoke from the man's nickel see-gar.

The seven children were squeezed into the truck bed with them, the bigger ones sitting with slumped shoulders to accommodate themselves to its low canvas cover. They were all around them, shielding them from view, hiding them as effectively as though they had been at the bottom of a well. But close as they were physically, they were still worlds apart.

Carol smiled at one of the girls, and received a flat stare in return. She started to pat the tot's head, and barely jerked her hand back in time to

146

avoid being bitten. The eldest boy protectively took charge of the child. 'Wouldn't do that no more, ma'am,' he advised Carol with chill politeness. 'He don't cotton none to strangers.'

The truck's best speed was barely thirty miles an hour. Despite their early starts and late stops, they seldom made two hundred miles a day. Their food was monotonously unvaried, practically the same from one meal to the next. Salt pork and gravy, biscuits or mush, and chicory coffee for breakfast. For lunch, mush or biscuits and salt pork eaten cold while they rode. And for dinner, there was more biscuits, and pork and gravy, with perhaps some sweetnin' (sorghum) and a poke salad – greens boiled with pork into a greasy, tasteless mess.

Doc ate heartily of everything. Nauseated by the stuff, Carol ate no more than she had to to stay alive. She acquired a painful and embarrassing stomach complaint. Her small body ached constantly from the jouncing and bouncing of the truck. She became very bitter of Doc; the more so because she knew her predicament was her own fault, and because she dared not complain.

These people didn't like her. They tolerated her only because she was Doc's woman (his *woman*, for Pete's sake!). And without Doc, she would be lost.

Whether the family knew who they were – the most wanted criminals in the country – is a moot point. But reading no newspapers, having no radio, living in their own close-mouthed world of existing to exist, it is unlikely that they did. And probably they would have turned their back on the opportunity to inform themselves.

These folks was feedin' them. These folks' business was their own business.

Ask no questions an' you'll hear no lies.

Curiosity killed the cat.

Leave well enough be, an' you'll be well enough.

The old truck limped westward, carrying Doc and Carol far beyond the danger zone of road-blocks and police checks, and into the whilom safety of California. And there, after another day or so of travel, they parted company with the family.

Doc didn't want them to know his and Carol's destination, to get any closer to it than they already were. That would be asking for trouble, and asked-for trouble was usually gotten. More-over, the family did not wish to go any farther south – into an area that was traditionally hostile to vagrants or anyone who might possibly become vagrant. And they hoped to have other fish to fry, or rather, apples to pick in the Pacific Northwest.

So there were monosyllabic farewells, a final exchange of money; then the family moved on, and Carol and Doc remained behind . . . Quite inappropriately in the City of Angels.

Doc was dressed in blue overalls and a jumper, and a striped railroad worker's cap. He carried himself with a pronounced stoop; a pair of

148

old-fashioned steel-rimmed glasses were perched on the end of his nose, and he peered over them nearsightedly as he paid for his ticket from a snap-top money pouch. A metal lunch basket was tucked under one arm. Beneath his clothes – and Carol's – was an outsize money belt.

Carol came into the railroad station several minutes after him. She also was stooped, crone-like of figure. She wore a long, shapeless black dress, and under the shadow of her head shawl her face was wizened and sunblack.

They boarded the train separately. Carol taking a rear seat, Doc entering the men's lounge. Then, when their tickets had been collected and the train was well out of the yards, he came out and sat down at her side.

He opened the lunch bucket and took out a pint bottle of whiskey. He drank from it thirstily, wiped the neck with his sleeve, and extended it toward Carol.

She shook her head, her nose wrinkling dis-tastefully. 'Do you have to keep hitting that stuff?' she frowned.

"Keep hitting it?' He returned her frown. 'That's the first drink I've had in days.'

'Well, it's one too many at a time like this! If you ask me, I . . .'

'But I didn't.' He took another long drink, then returned the bottle to the lunch bucket. 'Look,' he said reasonably. 'What do you want to do anyway? Break up? Go it on your own? I'd like to know.'

'As if you didn't already know! What the hell difference does it make what I want to do?'

'Well,' said Doc. 'Well, then.'

Actually, he did not want to be separated from her. Even if it had been practical, he would not have wanted it. And despite anything she said or did, he knew that she felt the same way. They were still in love – as much as they had ever been. Strangely, nothing had changed that.

His eyes drifted shut. He wondered where the family of share-croppers was by now, and subconsciously he wished that he was still with them. It hadn't been at all bad, that long creeping journey across half of the United States. Nothing to do but ride and ride, with every day exactly like the one before. No worries, no decisions to make. Above all the freedom, in fact the necessity, *not* to talk.

He had never before realized the blessedness of silence – the freedom to be silent, rather, if one chose. He had never realized, somehow, that such blessedness might be his privilege. He was Doc McCoy, and Doc McCoy was born to the obligation of being one hell of a guy. Persuasive, impelling of personality; insidiously likable and good-humored and imperturbable. One of the nicest guys you'd ever meet, that was Doc McCoy. They broke the pattern when they made him. And, of course, Doc *did* like people and he liked to be liked. And he'd been well compensated for his efforts in that direction. Still – well, there you were. It had become an effort, something else that he hadn't realized.

Maybe he was just very tired, he thought wearily. And very worried. Because exactly what they were going to do after they got to Golie's, he didn't know.

'Doc,' Carol said. 'What's the next step, after we get to Golie's?'

Doc grimaced. She can read my mind, he thought. 'I'm thinking about it,' he said. 'I haven't decided, yet.'

'You don't know, do you? You haven't any plan.'

'Now, that's putting it a little strong. I'll have to check around, and –' her scornful smile stopped him. 'All right,' he said, 'I don't know.'

She waited, staring at him demandingly. He fumbled the lunch bucket open and took another drink. He gestured with it diffidently, then quickly recapped it and put it away.

'I – it would have been simple enough ordinarily,' he explained. 'I mean, if we could have made it before they had the alarm out for us. Coming back from Mexico, you're apt to get a pretty thorough going over. But going over, they hardly take a second look at you. You can just walk across the border, or drive across and . . .'

'All right! But that's what we *could* have done!'

'Well – maybe we still can. There doesn't seem to be much noise out here about us. Maybe . . .'

He broke off, unable to continue so palpable

151

a lie. Perhaps there wasn't any general search for them on the West Coast, but the border patrol would certainly have been alerted.

'We'll see,' he mumbled. 'I'll have to look around. Maybe I can get a line on Ma Santis.'

'Ma Santis!' Carol let out a disgusted snort. 'Just like that you're going to get a line on Ma Santis, huh? You already told me you thought she was dead, and even if she wasn't I'd like to know how you're going to get a line on her or anyone else. You can't make any inquiries. You can't go wandering around and . . .'

'That's right. I can't,' Doc said curtly; and he got up and entered the rest room.

Seated on the long leather couch, he lighted a cigarette, looked wearily out into the moonlit night. He had always thought this was the most beautiful stretch of country in the world, this area of orange and avocado groves, of rolling black-green hills, of tile-roofed houses – all alike yet all different – stretching endlessly along the endless expanse of curving, white-sand beach. He had thought about retiring here some day and though the idea was preposterous, he still thought about it. He could see himself and Carol on the patio of one of those incredibly gay houses. Barbecuing a steak perhaps, or sipping tall drinks while they stared out to sea. There would be a cool breeze blowing in, temperately cool and smelling of salt. And . . .

'Doc —' Carol murmured suddenly from the doorway.

He said, 'Coming,' and rejoined her in the seat. And she patted his hand and gave him a lingering smile.

'You know something, Doc?' she whispered. 'This will be our first night together. Our first night together and alone.'

'So it will!' Doc made his voice hearty. 'It doesn't seem possible, does it?'

'And I'm not going to let anything spoil it either. Nothing! We'll just pretend like we don't have a worry in the world tonight. Just push everything out of our minds and have ourselves a nice long hot bath, and something to eat and – and . . .'

She squeezed his hand. Almost fiercely.

'Sandy-Egg-O!' bawled the conductor. 'Next stop is San Diego!'

CHAPTER TWELVE

The cabdriver accepted Doc's tip with a grunt of surprise; he'd figured this pair for stiffs and maybe even no-pays. They were some kind of foreigners, he guessed, and they didn't know their way around yet. And he hastened to place himself at their disposal.

'Maybe you folks would like to go somewhere for a bite to eat?' he suggested. 'After you, uh, get cleaned up a little, I mean.'

'Well –' Doc glanced at Carol. 'I'm not sure just how long we'll . . .'

'Or I could bring you something if you don't want to go out. Sandwiches, chicken an' French fries, maybe some Chinese or Mexican food. Anything you say, beer, booze, or baloney, and no service charge. Just my cab fare and waitin' time.'

'Suppose you wait a moment,' Doc said. 'I'll have to see about a cabin.'

Fat little Golie was nervous, but then Golie almost always was; he had things to make him that way. So Doc couldn't say just what it was that made him feel uneasy. He stalled over the selection of a cabin, finally choosing one at the far end of the court. But his effort to smell out the trouble he felt, to get at the source of his hunch, was unavailing.

Leaving the office, he gave the cabdriver his cabin number and a twenty; ordered two chicken dinners, cigarettes and a carton of coffee. The cabdriver saluted and sped away, and Doc and Carol went down the long single row of cabins to the last one.

He unlocked the door, switched on the light.

Carol yanked down the shade, pirouetted, and flopped down on the bed, kicking her legs high into the air. 'Boy,' she breathed. 'Does this ever feel good!' Then, wiggling her finger at him, 'Come here you! Right this minute!'

Doc took a step toward her, then stopped short, frowning. 'Listen! Do you hear anything?'

'Oh, now, Doc. Of course, I hear something. After all, we're not the only people in the court.'

Doc stared at her absently, his brow furrowed with thought. Carol jumped up and put her arms around him. Leaned into him, smiling into his face. This was to be their night together, didn't he remember? Their first night in more than four years. So would he kindly stop acting foolish and jumpy, and . . .

'That's it!' Doc's eyes narrowed suddenly. 'Golie's family! There was none of 'em around, didn't you notice? Not even that overstuffed wife of his, and she hasn't been twenty feet away from the place since she came here. We've

155

got to get out of here, Carol! Now!'

'G-get out? But – but . . .'

'He's sent them away somewhere, don't you see? He must have! And there's only one reason why he would have.'

'But –' Carol looked at him incredulously. 'But why? What could . . .'

'I don't know! It doesn't matter! It may be too late already, but . . .'

It was too late. There was a crunch of gravel outside. Then a polite knock on the door, and woman's soft voice.

'Mr Kramer? Miz' Kramer?'

Doc stiffened, whipped a gun from beneath the bib of his overalls. He gripped Carol's arm, held it for a moment, then nodded to her.

'Yes?' Carol called. 'Who is it, please?'

'The maid, ma'am. I brought you some towels.'

Doc glanced into the bathroom, and slowly shook his head. He pointed at Carol's dress, mouthed a silent speech.

'Could you just leave them on the step, please? I'm undressed.'

There was silence for a long moment, a whispering so faint that it might have been anything but a whisper. But that was the tip-off. There was someone with this maid, if it was a maid. Someone who was giving her instructions.

Doc looked around swiftly. He squeezed Carol's arm again and pointed toward the bathroom, and his lips formed the word 'Window'. Carol shook her head violently and tried to hang onto him;

156

then winced and nodded whitely as he gave her arm another painful squeeze.

He raised the window silently. He heard the maid say, 'I can't leave 'em outside, ma'am. Maybe your husband can come and get 'em.'

'Just a moment, please,' Carol called back. 'He's in the bathroom right now.'

Doc dropped through the window. He tiptoed along the rear of the house and around the side, and peered carefully around the corner.

Rudy! The gun in his hand jerked involuntarily. How in the hell!

He put it out of his mind; the wonderment, the sense of being unbearably put upon. Facts were facts, something to be accepted and dealt with, and the fact was that Rudy was here.

There was a woman with him – it was Fran Clinton – but she didn't appear to be armed. Gun in hand, Rudy stood to one side of her, his head turned away from Doc.

He didn't want to use the gun, of course. He could no more afford a racket than Doc and Carol could. His objective and Doc's would be exactly the same – to settle their score silently and unseen in the privacy of the cabin.

Doc hefted his gun, raised the barrel level with his shoulder. He edged silently around the corner of the building.

Rudy first – with one skull-crushing blow from the gun. Then, before the woman could move or yell, a hard left hook with his free hand.

Eyes fixed on them, Doc slowly raised and

lowered his foot. It came down on an up-cornered brick, one of several that had once formed the border of a flower bed. And he fell headlong.

Falling, he triggered the gun; it was all he could do now.

Instantly Rudy whirled, gun blazing, whirling the woman in front of him. But his bullets passed above Doc, and Doc's drilled through the woman and into him.

And in seconds they lay dead on the ground, one of Rudy's hands still holding her arm behind her back.

From a couple of blocks away, the cabdriver heard the racket. But he did not place it as coming from Golie's, and certainly he did not connect it with his recent fares. Then he saw Doc and Carol running down the street toward him – *and, hey! Look at the old gal run, would you?* – and puzzled he stopped the cab and got out.

'Somethin' wrong, folks? Somebody givin' you some trouble?'

'Yes,' Doc told him. 'I'll explain it while you're driving us into the city.'

'Into Diego? But what about your grub? What...'

Doc jabbed a gun into his stomach, gave him a shove toward the cab. 'Do you want to go on living? Do you? Then do what I tell you!'

The driver obeyed, but sullenly. With the dragging deliberation of the very stubborn. As they reached the highway and turned toward town, he gave Doc a self-righteous glare.

'This won't get you nothin', Mac,' he said. 'I don't know what you're after, but this won't get you a thing.'

Doc looked at him, tight-lipped. In the back seat, Carol leaned forward anxiously. 'Doc – I think he's right. There's probably an alert out for us already. Golie'll spill everything now. How far can we get in this circus wagon?'

Doc asked her curtly how far they would get without it. With an alert on the air, what chance did they have of grabbing another car? 'The cops won't know what we're traveling in. Or whether we're traveling in anything. Maybe we can make it to the border before they find out.'

'*To* the border! But what . . .'

'You'll never do it, Mac,' the driver cut in doggedly. 'The best thing you can do is give yourselves up. Now – *oof*!'

'Like it?' Doc gave him another prod with the gun. 'Want some more?'

Teeth gritted, the man shook his head.

'All right, then,' Doc said mildly. 'Make a left here, and head straight up Mission Valley until I tell you to turn.'

The cab swung left. They sped down the curving, cliff-shadowed road, and after a time Doc spoke over his shoulder to Carol. They couldn't get through the border gates, he said. That, obviously, would be impossible. But they might be able to slip across the line at some unguarded point.

'People do it all the time,' he went on. 'It's

not the best bet in the world, and we'll still have problems if and when we get across, but . . .'

'You won't make it,' the driver broke in, dogged again. 'Not anywhere near the gates where you'll be tryin'. I know that border, mister, and I'm telling you . . .'

His sentence ended in a scream. The cab swerved, and he turned pain-crazed eyes on Doc. 'You t-try that again!' he gasped. 'You do that again and see what happens!'

Doc promised that he wouldn't do it again. 'Next time I'll shoot you. Now go right at this next turn. We're hitting crosstown to the Tijuana highway.'

The cab made the turn with an angry skidding of tires. They raced up the steep road into Mission Hills, then down the long arterial street which skirts San Diego's business district. The traffic began to thicken. There was the wail of a siren – fading eerily into the distance.

Above the windshield the blurred murmuring of the radio squawk box became a crisp voice:

'Cab Seventy-nine! Cab Seventy-nine! Come in, Seventy-nine . . .'

The driver was elaborately disinterested. Doc glanced at the identification plate on the instrument panel, and spoke to him sharply. 'That's you. Answer it!'

'What d'you want me to say?'

'Tell her you've got a couple of people on a sightseeing tour. You'll be tied up for about an hour.'

160

'Sightseeing tour?' The driver squirmed into the seat, leaned slightly over the wheel. 'She won't never go for that mister. She'll know I got a couple of crooks headin' for Tijuana.'

'Wh-at?' Doc frowned. 'How will she know?'

'She just will. She'll even know where we are right now. Just making the turnoff for National City.'

Doc got it then. He linked the driver's seemingly senseless speech with a breathless silence of the squawk box. And savagely, his nerves worn raw, he smashed the gun barrel into the man's stubborn, doughish face.

He smashed it; he smashed it again. The driver groaned and flung himself against the door of the car. It shot open, and he went tumbling and bouncing into the street.

The door swung shut again. Doc fought the wheel of the cab, swinging it out of the path of an oncoming vehicle. There was a frozen silence from Carol; a wondering silence. Then, answering her unspoken question, the voice of the squawk-box:

'Seventy-nine? Seventy-nine – I read you, Seventy-nine . . .'

Doc found the switch and closed it.

He turned off the highway, sped along roughly parallel to it on a gravel country road.

He asked, 'Is there a radio back there?' And Carol said there was none.

It didn't matter, of course. They both knew what would be happening by now.

The county road got them around National City. Then, implacably, it veered back toward the highway.

Doc tried to get away from it. Lights turned off, he waved the cab through a network of outlying side streets. That got them only a little farther south, and in the end they were led back to the highway. Doc stopped just short of it, his mind racing desperately to the lazy throb of the cab's motor.

Take to the fields – run for it on foot? No, no, it was too late. As impractical and impossible as trying to hook another car.

Well, then, how about – how about moving in on one of these suburbanites? Holing up with them, holding the family hostage until there was a chance to make a break for it?

No again. Not with them penned in in so small an area. Holing up would simply eliminate the almost no-chance they had now.

Doc shrugged unconsciously. He watched the intermittent flash of lights in front of them, listened to the *swish-flick* of the cars speeding past the intersection. And finally, since there was nothing else to do, he drove back onto the highway again.

Other cars whipped past them, and laughter, snatches of happy conversation spilled out into the night. Pleasure seekers; people in a hurry to begin their evening of wining and dining across the border, and with nothing more to fear than a hangover in the morning.

162

People who had *earned* their good time.

Doc drove slowly. For once in his life, he had no plan. He saw no way out. They could not turn back. Neither could they cross the border, through the gates or any other way.

The police had only to wait for them. To close in the net until they were snared in it.

After time he turned off the highway again, pursuing a winding trail until it came to a dead end by the ocean. He backed up headed back in the direction from which he had come. And then he was again on the highway, moving south.

The other cars were not moving so quickly now. They shot past the cab, then a few hundred yards beyond they began to slow. And peering into the distance, Doc saw why.

So did Carol; and she spoke for the first time in minutes. Spoke with a tone that was at once angry, frightened, and a little gleeful. 'Well, Doc. What do you figure on doing now?'

'Do?'

'The roadblock. What are you going to do?' Her voice broke crazily. 'Just drive on into it? Just keep on going, and say yessir, I'm D-Doc McCoy, and th-this is my wife, Carol, and – a-and . . .'

'Shut up!' Doc cut in. 'Look!'

'Don't you tell me t-to – look at what?'

'Just ahead of us there. That thing at the side of the road.'

It seemed to be suspended some six feet above the roadside embankment, an illuminated oblong blob topped by a larger and shadowy blob. Then,

163

as the cab crept toward it, the outlines of the two blobs became clearer, revealed themselves as a woman's face beneath a man's hat.

She was holding a flashlight in her hand, shining the beam into her face. Swinging loosely from her other hand was a shotgun. A raw-boned giant of a woman, she wore overalls and sheepkin coat. She stared at them – at the cab rather; flicked the beam of the flashlight across it.

Then she made a brief swinging motion with it, the light disappeared, and so did she.

Doc let out a suppressed shout. He glanced over his shoulder quickly, waited for the two cars behind him to pass.

Carol shook him fiercely. 'Doc, what's the matter with you? Who – what was that?' And Doc laughed a little wildly, babbled that he couldn't believe it himself. And then he slammed the cab into low gear, cut the wheels to the right, and went roaring up over the embankment and into the field.

It was wasteland, an expanse of eroded top-soilless rock. Ahead of them, the tall shadow of the woman beckoned, then moved away swiftly, guided them up over a rise in the land and down into a cuplike valley.

There was a house there, a dark, deserted-looking shack. Two great forms came bounding from behind it – mastiffs – and streaked toward the cab in deadly silence. But the woman spoke, gestured to them, and they came meekly to heel. Trotted along with her as she strode past the shack, and on into the darkness beyond it.

'Doc! Do you hear me? I want to know what this is all about!'

Doc didn't answer her. It was in his mind perhaps that he had already explained fully; and all his thoughts now were on the woman and the deliverance which she represented.

About a hundred yards beyond the house, she came to a stop; turned and faced them, beckoned them forward slowly until they were almost upon her. Then she stopped them with a pushing motion of her hand and yanked open the door of the cab. 'Got anything in here that you want to save, Doc? Well, pile out then. We're gettin' rid of it for good.'

They piled out. Just back of the point where the woman had been standing was a broad crater, the dull gleam of moonlight on dark water.

'Gravel pit,' the woman explained succinctly. 'Ain't got no bottom to it that I ever found. Now, we'll just give this buggy a good hard push . . .'

They pushed, straining, then trotting sluggishly as the cab gathered speed. Then, at a warning grunt from the woman, they came to a halt. And the cab shot over the brink of the pit, descended with a resounding splash and disappeared beneath the oily surface.

The woman turned and gripped Doc's hand. 'Doc, you're a sight for sore eyes, and that's a fact. Couldn't hardly believe it was you when I got the word on the radio tonight.'

'And you, needless to say, are also a sight for

sore eyes,' Doc murmured. 'You were waiting for us down there on the highway?'

'Yep. Knew you was headin' this way. Just took a chance on you spotting me. Incidentally,' her voice altered slightly, 'not that I really give a whoop, but what happened between you and Rudy?'

'Well—' Doc hesitated. 'You know Rudy. He never was quite right in the head and he'd gotten a lot worse. The more reasonable you tried to be with him, why . . .'

'Yeah, sure. Finally blew his top, huh? Well, I been expecting it for a long time.' The woman shook her head wisely. 'But to hell with the poor devil. Right now we got to hide you an' – and . . .'

She paused with rough delicacy, glancing at Carol.

Doc apologized hastily. 'I'm sorry. Ma – Mrs Santis – I'd like you to meet my wife, Carol.'

It is scarcely to be wondered at that Carol's handshake had been a little limp. She had heard so much of this gaunt, craggy-faced woman for so long that she had almost come to regard her as a myth.

Ma Santis. Daughter of a criminal, wife of a criminal, mother of six criminal sons. Two of Ma's boys had died in gun battles with the police; two others – like their father – had died in the electric chair. Of the remaining two, one was in jail, and the other, Earl, was at liberty. The

166

Santises were hill people, rebels and outlaws rather than criminals in the usual sense of the word. They never forgot a favor nor forgave an injury. They were that rare thing in the world of crime, people with a very real sense of honor. In another era, they might have been pirates or privateers or soldiers of fortune. It was their misfortune and perhaps the nation's as a whole that they had been born into a civilization which insisted upon conformity and pardoned no breakage of its laws, regardless of one's needs or motives.

The Santises were unable to conform. They would have died, and did die, rather than attempt to. And now at age sixty-four, and after more than twenty years in prison, Ma was as completely unreconstructed as she had been at fourteen.

Her son Earl was living over in the back country, she explained. Doin' enough farming to look respectable, and livin' high on the hog from cached loot. 'Been so long since me or him turned a trick that people plumb forgot all about us,' Ma chuckled. 'So I figures we'll probably get a good goin' over here at my place, but no more'n t'any other. You just hole up where I put you until Earl shows up, an' – by the by, you was headin' for El Rey's, Doc?'

'That's right.'

'Well, don't you never doubt you'll make it,' Ma said firmly. 'Me'n Earl, we helped plenty of friends to get there – Pat Gangloni, Red Reading, Ike Moss an' his woman. 'Course, you're maybe a little hotter'n any of them, but – come here.'

She turned and went back to the brink of the pit; squatted there, pointing with the beam of her flashlight. 'You see that? Them two clumps of bushes? Now look right below them, there at them kind of shady places just under the water line.'

'I see them,' Doc nodded. 'Caves?'

'You could call 'em that. Really ain't much more than holes. Just about big enough to crawl into and get out of sight, but that's all you need, ain't it?' Ma laughed jovially.

Doc hesitated, shooting a quick glance at Carol's taut face. 'It – you think this is necessary, Ma? I mean . . .'

'Wouldn't have you do it if I didn't think so.' There was a hint of tartness in her voice. 'It ain't so bad, Doc. There's fresh air seeps in from somewhere, and it ain't really so cramped. Pat Gangloni took it, and you know Pat. Makes two fellas your size with half a man left over.'

Doc forced himself to laugh at the joke. 'We'll have to strip, I suppose?'

'I'd say so. Unless you want to keep on your unmentionables. They's blankets down there, an' it's kind of hot anyways.'

'Fine,' Doc said. 'Well . . .'

He unbuttoned his jumper and dropped it to the ground. He sat down and began taking off his shoes and socks. Ma looked at Carol. She said, 'Prob'ly need a rope,' and disappeared into the darkness.

Carol remained standing, motionless, making no move to remove her clothes.

'Carol,' Doc said. Then, 'Carol!'

'No-no,' Carol said shakily. 'No, I can't! How do I know that – that . . .'

'You're with me. You're riding on my ticket. Now get out of those clothes!'

He stood up, stripped out of the jeans. He unbuckled the money belt and dropped it on top of the pile of clothing. He waited a moment, working up an encouraging smile, storing up warmth for his voice. Then, hand outstretched, he took a step toward Carol.

She backed desperately away from him. 'N-no! No!' she gasped. 'I know what you're planning! You'll get me down there and . . .'

'Stop it! What else can you do, anyway?'

'I know you! I'd never get back up again! She's your friend, not mine! She – y-you'd leave me down there under the ground and . . .'

'Well, here we are.' Ma Santis was suddenly back with them. 'Trouble?'

'I'm sorry,' Doc said. 'My wife's a little upset.'

'Uh-huh,' Ma drawled. 'Thought she kind of sounded like she was. Me, I'm just a leetle upset myself. Figures I was goin' a long ways to do you two a favor, and now I ain't so sure. Like to get set straight before I go any farther.'

Doc repeated that he was sorry. Ma shifted the shotgun under her arm, and behind her the two mastiffs suddenly came to attention. She

169

waited, staring stonily at Carol. And as if from some great distance, Carol heard her own voice; felt her face stiffen in a conciliatory smile.

She was sorry. She hadn't meant what she said. She was grateful to Ma. She . . .

She broke off, stooping to pull the voluminous black dress over her head. Almost eagerly she unfastened the money belt, made a tentative gesture of offering it to the older woman. Ma motioned laconically with the gun. 'Just drop it on the pile. An' don't worry about none of it showin' up missing.'

'You help yourself to as much as you want,' Doc said warmly. 'I mean that, Ma. We . . .'

Ma nodded. She knew he meant it, but she wasn't needin' nothing. 'Always thought you was a hell of a guy, Doc. Heard a thing or two to the contrary, but you was always square with me an' mine. Ain't a one of us that didn't think the world of you.'

'And I've felt exactly the same way about all of you, Ma.'

'But,' she continued, 'I ain't buyin' in on no one else's fight. I ain't putting myself any further in the middle than I am already. You two got a quarrel, which I hope you ain't, you settle it somewhere else. Elsewise, I'll do the settlin' and it won't be no fun for the party that starts the trouble.'

She paused, looking from one to the other, waiting for their acknowledgements of her statement. Carol's was somewhat readier than Doc's.

'Well, that's fine,' Ma said mildly. 'Now there's some water in them holes; prob'ly a little stale but you can drink it if you're thirsty enough. No grub, o' course. You can do without for as long as you're down there. No smokin' and no matches; ain't enough air to allow it. Well, that about does it, I guess. Want me to help you down, Doc?'

Doc shook his head. 'I can make it all right, thanks. Have you any idea how long it will be, Ma?'

'Well, I'd say tomorrow night. But you know how it is, Doc. Come see, come sah.' She laughed throatily. 'Oh, yeah, I knew I was forgettin' something. Sleepin' pills. Can't tell you where they are exactly, but just feel around an' you'll find 'em.'

'Oh, fine. I was just going to ask about them. Now, if you'll just give me a little light for a moment, Ma . . .'

Ma squatted again, beamed the flashlight down the wall of the pit. Doc studied it, gave her shoulder a pat of thanks, and poised himself on the brink.

'Good night,' he said, and shooting a smile at Carol, 'and a very good night to you, my dear.'

Then he jumped, stiff-legged.

There was an audible grunt as he struck the water.

He went under, and he came up. And then, getting a grip on the bushes, he pushed himself under again.

171

And stayed under.

'Now, there,' Ma said quietly, 'there is one hell of a guy. Just in case you didn't know it.'

'I know it,' Carol said.

She took the rope that Ma handed her, took a turn around her waist with it. Bellying down on the ground, she got her legs over the edge of the pit and squirmed slowly backward. She paused there, half-suspended in space, breathing very rapidly. Then she looked up and gave Ma the nod to lower her.

'Got somethin' on your mind.' Ma held her where she was for a moment. 'Maybe you better unload it while you can.'

'I – nothing, I guess. I was just going to ask about the sleeping pills. I mean, why you and Doc seem to take it for granted that we'll need them.'

'Why?' Ma frowned incredulously. 'Hey, you ain't been around much, have you, honey?'

'Well – I used to think so.'

'Uh-huh,' Ma said. 'Mmm-hum. Well, I'll tell you somethin' about them pills. Don't you doubt that you'll need 'em. An' don't wait to take 'em until you do. You gulp you down some right to begin with, an' when them wears off . . .'

She tugged upward on the rope, then slacked off on it. Carol swung off at the brink, and moved slowly down toward the water.

'Yes?' she called, shivering as her feet touched the water. 'When they begin to wear off?'

'Take some more,' Ma said.

The hole lay on a slant and for its first two or three feet it was largely filled with water, making it all but impossible to breathe until one had navigated it.

Carol came through it at a frantic scramble; continued to scramble forward with eyes closed, breath held, until her head butted against the rock at the end of the hole. And then gratefully, gasping in the air, she let herself go prone.

Strangely, it was not absolutely dark. Wherever the faint seepage of air came from, there was an equally faint seepage of light, if only the relative light of the night outside, to relieve the blackness of this hidden cave.

It was like being in a coffin, she thought. A dimly lit, well-ventilated coffin. It wasn't uncomfortable; not yet at least. Merely confining. As long as one was content to remain in it, and did not try to get out . . .

Abruptly, she cut off the thought.

Fumbling in the dimness, running her hands up to the end of the hole, she encountered the oval canvas-covered surface of a water canteen. She shook it, felt the swish and swing of the liquid inside. She laid it down again and continued to fumble until she found a small tightly capped bottle. She got the cap off and sniffed the contents. Taking out one of the capsules, she pinched it and touched her tongue to it.

Mildly bitter; a faintly salty taste. She dropped it back into the bottle and screwed the lid back on.

She didn't need that stuff. She wasn't going to

take anything that made her any more helpless than she was already. Ma had told her, in so many words, that she had nothing to fear. She and Doc were both under Ma's protection, until they struck out on their own again. But just the same, she wasn't knocking herself out with goof balls. Ma might be absolutely on the square. She might be. But Doc could outsmart someone like her, without even halfway trying. And if he decided to have things his own way, and if he thought it was safe – well, never mind. But no sleeping pills for her.

If they *were* sleeping pills.

Her mind moved around and around the subject, moving with a kind of fuzzy firmness. With no coherent thought process, she arrived at a conviction – a habit with the basically insecure; an insecurity whose seeds are invariably planted earlier, in under- or over-protectiveness, in a distrust of parental authority which becomes all authority. It can later, with maturity – a flexible concept – be laughed away, dispeled by determined clear thinking. Or it can be encouraged by self-abusive resentment and brooding self-pity. It can grow ever greater until the original authority becomes intolerable, and a change becomes imperative. Not to a radical one in thinking; that would be too troublesome, too painful. The change is simply to authority in another guise which, in time, and under any great stress, must be distrusted and resented even more than the first.

Thrashing it – and herself – Carol wondered why she feared Doc as she did – how she could fear him and be unable to trust him. And yet love him as she could never love another.

Even now, despite her fear and distrust, she would have given anything to have him with her.

He was always, or virtually always, so calm and self-assured. He always knew just what to do, and how to do it. He could be breaking apart inside and you'd never know it from the way he acted. He'd be just as pleasant and polite as if he didn't have a care in the world. You had to be careful with someone like that. You could never know what he was thinking. But . . .

She sighed uxoriously, squirming a little. Doc McCoy – one hell of a guy, Ma had called him. And that had seemed to say it all.

There just wasn't anyone else in the world like Doc, and there never would be.

She toyed with the bottle of pills. Then, turning on her side, she tapped on the wall with it. He couldn't be too far away from her, just a few feet through this coldly sweating rock. If she could make him hear her, and if he would reply to it – well, it would be nice. Each would be comforted, she persuaded herself, to know that the other was all right.

She tapped and listened. Tapped and listened. She frowned, with a kind of angry nervousness. Then, brightening, she turned and tapped on the opposite wall. Perhaps he was there, on that side.

After all, he just about had to be, didn't he? He had to be on one side or the other.

She tapped and listened. Tapped and listened.

The silence between tappings pressed in around her. It became an aching thing, a void crying to be filled. It was unbearable, and since the unbearable cannot be borne, her imagination, that friendly enemy, stepped in.

Quite clearly, she heard Doc's answering taps. Well, not clearly perhaps – the imagination does have its limitations – but she did hear them.

She tapped and he – it – tapped. The signals went back and forth. A great relief spread through her; and then, on its heels, overlaying it, an increasing restlessness and irritation.

What was the point in just tapping, in just making a meaningless noise? Now, if she could send him a message. Ask him, tell him to – to . . .

But maybe he'd already thought of that. And thought it was impossible. And maybe it was.

She pushed herself back against the wall, then measured the space to the opposite wall. There seemed to be enough room, for two people, that is. It could get to be a tight squeeze, of course, you couldn't continue it indefinitely. But just for a little while, an hour or so, it would be fine.

The overhead space? Well. She placed her palms against the roof of the hole, gave a start at its nearness to her. In the dimness it had seemed much farther away. She pushed on it, not realizing that she was pushing. And suddenly she pounded on it with her fists.

She stopped that very quickly, and lay very still for a few minutes until the wild pounding of her heart had stopped. Then, pushing herself with heels and elbows, she began to scoot toward the entrance.

Water touched her feet. She jerked them away from it. She let them slide into it again, and remain there for a moment. And then with resentful resignation she withdrew them. For obviously she couldn't leave this place, go back out into the pit. Someone might see her. For all she knew, the place might be swarming with cops by this time. At any rate, the water was very deep – bottomless, Ma had said – and she could swim very little. If she should be unable to find the hole Doc was in, or if she was unable to get into it or get back into this one . . .

Perhaps *they* had planned it that way. *They* hoped and expected that she would try to leave, knowing that she would drown if she did.

But, anyway, leaving was out of the question. She had to stay here until she was got out, as – her pendulum mind swinging back again – she assured herself she would be. Doc would get her out. After all, she was his wife and they'd been through a lot together, and she'd done a lot for him. And – and – if he'd really wanted to get rid of her, he'd had plenty of chances before this.

He'd get her out all right, as soon as it was safe.

Ma would make him.

It was just a little roomier, down here near the entrance to the hole. The roof was just a little higher. She measured the distance with her upstretched palms, thinking that there was almost room enough to sit up. And no sooner had the thought entered her mind than she knew she must sit up.

She had to. She could not remain prone, or lie half-propped up on her elbows another minute.

Tucking her chin against her chest, she raised herself experimentally. Six inches, a foot, a foot and a half, a – the stone pressed against her head. She shoved against it stubbornly, then with a suppressed 'Ouch!' she dropped back to the floor.

She rested for a moment, then tried again. A kind of sideways try this time, with her knees pulled upward. That got her up a little farther, though not nearly far enough. But it did – or seemed to – show her how the trick could be done.

She was very lithe and limber, more so now than ever after the arduous thinning-down of their cross-country journey. So she sucked her stomach in, drew her knees flat against it, and pressed her chin down against them. And thus, in a kind of flat ball, she flung herself upward and forward.

Her head struck the roof with a stunning bump, then skidded along it gratingly, leaving a thin trail of hair and scalp. She would have stopped with the first painful impact, but the momentum of her body arced her onward. And then at last she was sitting up. Or rather, sitting, bent forward as she was, it would have been far from accurate to say that she was sitting up.

The roof pressed upon her neck and shoulders. Her head was forced downward. Her widespread legs were flatted against the floor, and, to support herself, she had her hands placed between them. She raised one of them to brush at her face, but the strain was so intolerable that she hastily put it back in use as a brace.

She rested, breathing heavily, finding it difficult to breathe at all in that constricting position; thinking, Well, at least I know I can do it now. I can sit up if I want to. Then, as the awkward pose became agonizing, she tried to lie down again. And was held almost motionless exactly as she was.

She couldn't accept the fact. It was too terrible. Now, surely, she thought, if I got into this, I can get out of it. If I can sit up, then I can s— I can lie down again.

'Of course I can,' she spoke, grunted, aloud. 'Why not, anyway?'

There was, of course, every reason why not. It was impossible to draw her legs up, as she had in the first instance. Almost impossible to move them at all. As for balling herself up – well, she already was; even more than she had been originally. But now there was no give in the ball. Her body was like an overburdened spring, so heavily laden that it can only go down farther and never up.

'No,' she said quietly. 'No.'

Then, on an ascending note, 'No, no, n-no!'

She waited, panting, the blood running to her head and her hair tumbled over her eyes. Her wrists throbbed, and her elbows arched with sugary pain. And suddenly they doubled under her and her torso lurched downward, and a tortured scream burbled from her lips.

Sobbing painfully, she braced herself again. Tears ran down her face, and she could not brush them away. And in her agony and growing hysteria, that seemed the most unbearable thing of all.

'C-can't – can't even raise a finger,' she wept. 'Can't even r-raise a . . .'

Then, so softly that she could hardly be heard, 'Ma said tomorrow night. Tomorrow night, prob'ly.'

The words trickled off into silence. Her panting grew more labored. She wheezed and coughed, groaned with the jerking of her body, and her tears ran harder.

'I – I can't – stand – *it!*' she gasped. 'You hear me? *I can't stand It!* Can't stand it, can't stand it, *c-caa-an't stand eet, can't stand ee-yaahhhhhh . . .*'

She screamed and the pain of the exertion caused her to scream even louder, and that scream wrung still another from her throat. She writhed and screamed, gripped in a frenzy of pain and fury. Her head pounded against the roof and her heels dug and kicked into the floor, and her elbows churned and banged and scraped against the imprisoning sides of the hole.

Blood mingled with the tears on her face. It streamed down her back, over her arms and legs and thighs. From a hundred tiny cuts and scratches and bruises it came, coating her body; warm red blood – combining slippery with the dust of the cave.

She never knew when she broke free. Or how. Or that she had. She was still struggling, still screaming, when she got the cap off the pill bottle and upended it into her mouth . . .

Peevishly, she came up out of the pleasant blackness. Something was gripping her ankle, and she tried to jerk away from it. But the thing held tight. It yanked, skidding her down the hole, peeling more hide from her body. She cried out in protest, and the cry was choked off suddenly as water closed over her.

Choking and kicking, she slid out of the hole and into the pit. It was night again – or night still? And in the moonlight, she looked blurrily into the flattest eyes she had ever seen.

'I'm Earl,' he grinned, showing twisted teeth. 'Just hold tight now, and I'll getcha . . .'

'Leggo!' She flung herself frantically backward. 'Just leave me alone! I don't want to go anywhere! P-please, please, don't make me! Just let me s-stay where . . .'

She made a grab for the bushes, tried to pull herself back into the hole. Treading water, Earl gave her a hard slap in the face.

'Son of a gun,' he mumbled, getting a rope around her waist, signaling to Ma and Doc. 'Wasn't forty-eight hours enough for yuh?'

CHAPTER THIRTEEN

Covered by odds and ends of sacking, Doc and Carol lay in the rear of Earl's old truck and were taken joltingly back through the hills to a country road, and thence on several miles to the so-called farm where Earl lived. It was a shabby, rundown place with a grassless junk-littered yard, a cow, a few chickens, a couple of acres of fruit trees and two or three more of truck crops. Inside the weatherbeaten house, however, with its bare warped floors and boarded-up windows, there was an outsize color TV set, a huge deep freeze and a refrigerator, and an enormous wood-fuel range.

Earl was obviously proud of these possessions, and Doc complimented him on them. Laconically, trying to conceal his pleasure, Santis took a large beef roast from the oven and slapped it platterless on the table. As he whacked it into great bleeding chunks, Ma set out other 'vittles' – cold boiled cabbage, bread, a pot of coffee, a gallon jug of bonded whiskey – and tin cups and plates. They all sat down then, and everyone but Carol began to eat hungrily. She sat dazed and listless, her stomach turning queasily, hardly able to tolerate the sight and the smell of the food.

Ma gave her an appraising look, and reached for the whiskey jug. She filled a tin cup – pronounced *tin*-cup – half full of the white liquid and thrust it across the table.

'Now, you drink that,' she ordered. 'Go on! Don't make me tell you twice.'

Carol drank it. She swallowed hastily, trying to swallow back the sickness, and then a comforting fire spread through her stomach, and a little color came back into her face.

'Now, eat,' Ma said. And Carol ate. And after the first few bites, the food tasted very good to her.

Both of her eyes were slightly blackened. Her mouth was puffy and bruised, and her face and hands were a mass of scratches and cuts. But no one commented on her appearance, or inquired into the why of it. Old hands in the sleazy bypaths of crime, they could pretty well guess what had happened to her.

She kept her eyes on the plate, taking no part in their conversation. As indifferent to it as though it had nothing to do with her.

Needless to say, she and Doc were still very hot. It would be impossible for them to sneak across the Mexican border, and make their way down into the interior by land. But Ma and Earl had lined up a good seaward contact

– the captain of a small Portuguese fisherman who had handled similar ventures for them before.

'No one with the kind of heat you two got, o'course.' Ma took a swig of whiskey, belched and wiped her mouth with the back of her hand. 'He's stallin' now, trying to weasel out of the deal. But he'll come around in a day or so, soon's he sees it ain't getting him nowheres.'

'You mean,' Doc frowned warily, 'you mean he knows who we are?'

Ma said sure, naturally the fellow knew. 'Who else would be skippin' the country right now? But don't you worry none about it, Doc. He knows all about us Santises, and you got nothing to worry about.'

'I see,' Doc said. 'Yes, I'm sure you're right.'

Roy Santis would be getting out of prison in another year or so. That would make three of them on the loose, not to mention their manifold kinsfolk and friends. And no one who was even slightly familiar with the Santis reputation would do anything to offend them. Anyone who did, in hope of reward or in fear of punishment, would never live to brag about it.

The meal over, Earl filled a crockery jug with water and led Carol and Doc down through his gullied backyard to a haystack-size mound of manure. It was partly dug out, roofed over with boards which were in turn covered with manure. Facing away from the house, the entrance was covered with a piece of canvas which was smeared

185

with cow dung, dried now but apparently applied when wet.

Diffidently Earl handed Doc the water jug. 'Get you some grub too, if you want it, Doc. Just figured you'd want to do your eatin' at night when you could come outside.'

'Of course,' Doc said. 'We won't want a thing now, Earl.'

'Well – oh, yeah. No smokin' – guess you don't need me to tell you that. Don't believe I'd even light a match if I was you. Little smoke or fire shows a long ways off.'

'I understand. There won't be any,' Doc promised.

'Ever chaw? Got an extra plug with me you can have.'

'Well, now, that might be all right,' Doc said. 'Thank you very much, Earl.'

Earl went back to the house. Doc politely held the canvas door aside, and waited for Carol to precede him.

It was an hour or so before dawn. Without a word, Carol curled up on the floor and was almost immediately asleep again. Doc hunkered down against the wall and took a chew of tobacco. He had slept himself out during the past two days and nights. Now sleeping was something to be done when he could no longer stay awake, something to be conserved against the boredom of wakefulness. He chewed and spat, carefully covering up the spittle each time. Occasionally he looked at the dark shadow that was Carol, and his eyes became brooding and thoughtful.

With the first rays of sunlight, the manure pile began to gather heat. By ten o'clock, when Carol came suddenly awake, Doc had stripped himself naked except for his shoes and socks, and was sitting cross-legged on his pile of clothes.

He shook his head warningly as she broke into startled laughter, then grinned in good-natured self-deprecation. 'Which would you say was the funniest?' he whispered. 'Me or the symbolism of the situation?'

'I can't decide.' She laughed softly. 'Maybe I'd better get into the act myself.'

She undressed, wiping away the sweat with her clothes, making a cushion of them as Doc had with his. And now that they were alone, Doc showed a great deal of concern about her many cuts and bruises. Carol made little of them; she deserved them, she said, for making a darned fool of herself. But she was pleased by his solicitude, and completely rested and relaxed, she felt very kindly toward him.

Head tilted to one side, she gave him an impish look. Then, leaning forward suddenly, she took his bristled face in her hands and . . .

A soggy mass struck her on the forehead, slid down across her face. She sat back abruptly, scrubbing and brushing at herself. 'Gaah!' she spat disgustedly, nose wrinkled. 'Ugh! Of all the filthy, messy . . .'

'Now, that was a shame,' Doc said, 'It's the heat,

I suppose. It softens this stuff up and . . .'

'Please!' She grimaced. 'Isn't it bad enough without you drawing me a picture?'

That was the end of any lovemaking. Doc withdrew behind the calm mask of his face, and Carol sank back into her former listlessness. As the long hours dragged by, she talked to herself silently; jeered the vague *they* and *them* for the fools that they were.

A lot of fun, isn't it? Oh, sure! Just like the movies. Real dramatic and exciting. Two big, bad, brainy bank robbers, hiding naked in a pile of manure!

The heat brought hordes of flies. It brought out swarms of corpse-colored grub worms, which dropped down on their heads and backs or crawled up under them from the floor. And it brought a choking, eye-watering stench, which seemed to seep through every pore of their skins.

Once, in desperation, Carol started to swing back the canvas door. But Doc pushed her away from it firmly. 'You know better than that. Try a chew of tobacco.'

'Tobacco? That'll kill the smell of this stuff?'

'No. But it'll take the taste of it out of your mouth.'

She hesitated, then held out her hand. 'Gimme. I can't be any sicker than I am already.'

She took a small chew. It did make her sicker, but it was a different kind of sickness, and even that was a relief.

She and Doc sat chewing and spitting, not bothering to cover the spittle, not having to. The manure dripped and plopped down on it. And the flies swarmed, and the bugs crawled. And so the long day dragged on, and at last it was night.

Earl carried several pails of water down from the house, and they were able to douse away some of the filth. But the stench and the tobacco-tainted taste of it remained with them. It flavored the little food they were able to eat; in their imagination they could even taste it in the whiskey which Earl served them from a hip-pocket bottle.

There was no one at the house, so Earl had to get back to it quickly. Which meant that Carol and Doc could not linger in the open as they had hoped to. Reluctantly they went back beneath the canvas door flap and into the wretchedness of another night. Doc settled himself down to as much comfort as he could create. Carol moved restlessly from one spot to another on the filthy floor.

Why? she whispered fiercely. Why did they have to be here? First those terrible underwater holes that even a rat would have run from and now this – this – place. It didn't make sense. After all, there'd been plenty of heat on them after they'd jumped the train, and they'd had to hide then. But never had they holed up in anything as bad as the Santises had provided.

'We were on the move then,' Doc pointed out

mildly. 'We weren't pinned down in so small an area.'

'I don't care! I say we could hide just as well in some place that we could at least *stand* – that was endurable, I mean.'

Doc said that they seemed to have endured thus far. Then, patiently, he went on to explain that the best hiding place was always the one which seemed utterly impossible for human habitation. The water holes, for example; as she had said, even a rat would have shied from them. And now the manure pile. If it was nauseously repellent even at a distance, who would expect anyone to take refuge inside of it?

Carol listened dully. Then ceased to listen. Or to think. She'd better not complain any more, she guessed. Her position was uncertain enough as it was. Unlike Doc, however, she had not schooled herself to accepting what she could not change, so she simply deadened herself to it. Lapsing into a blind, blank lifelessness where time was at one endless and nonexistent.

They were in the manure pile for two more nights and days.

On the third night, Earl came down to them without his usual burden of provisions.

'Grab yourself a bite at the house,' he explained. 'Get cleaned up, too. Looks like you're on your way.'

Earl lounged on the porch, his pack of vicious-looking curs romping around him. Seated around the kitchen table were Ma, the boat captain, Carol and Doc. Carol's hair was cut short to her head. Both she and Doc wore rolled-up stocking caps, jeans, and loosely fitting sweat shirts. To all appearances they were one with the captain's crew – his three kinsmen who stood behind his chair, beaming, frowning, smiling, as the case might be, in exaggerated imitation of his expression.

Right now they were all frowning.

'But twenty-five thousan'!' The captain rolled his eyes heavenward. 'What is twenty-five thousan' for such a risk? A mere pittance!'

'Then it ain't really the risk you mind,' Ma said drily, 'long as you get paid enough for it. That's the way it sizes up, Pete?'

'Well . . .'

'Sure it is. So you got a bigger risk, and you're gettin' bigger money. Twice what you ever got before. An' that's more'n fair, and it's all you're gonna get.'

The two money belts were on the table. Ma opened them, and counted out an equal amount from each.

Melodramatically, the captain continued his protests. 'It will not do, senhora! Me, I do not mind. We are old friends, an' with friends one is generous. But my crew—' he turned and shook his head at them. 'You see? They will not do it! They insis' that . . .'

'Who you kiddin'?' Ma laughed. 'Them ginks

191

don't even know what we're talkin' about.'

The captain scowled, then, his manner undergoing a complete change, he also laughed. 'Well, one must always try, yes? Even with friends, it is no less than a duty. But now that we are agreed . . .'

He reached for the money. Ma dropped a hamlike hand over it.

'When you get back,' she said. 'When I get the word from these people that they got to where they were goin', safe an' sound an' with all their belongings.'

'But – but,' the captain sputtered, coloring. 'You think I am stool pigeon? You do not trust me, yes?'

'Huh-uh. Didn't say nothin' like that.'

'Then why? An' suppose there is trouble? What if I could not come back, eh?'

'Then you wouldn't get no money. An',' she gave him a steady look, 'you wouldn't need none, Pete.'

His eyes fell. He mumbled weakly that the matter was really nothing to dispute about; he was quite content to wait for his money. Ma nodded, wadded the bills into a roll and tucked it into the front of her dress.

Earl came in from the porch. Everyone shook hands, and Doc suggested lightly that Ma and Earl come along on the journey. They demurred, grinning at each other as though exchanging some secret joke. 'Guess not, Doc. Me 'n Earl kind of likes it here.'

'Yeah,' said Earl. 'Yes, sir, we like it real well here.'

'An' o' course, we couldn't leave now, nohow. Not with Roy still in the pen.'

Doc said that he understood. There was an awkward moment of silence with no one seemingly able to speak or move. And then, prompted by something in Ma's attitude, Doc felt constrained to proffer payment for the help which she and Earl had rendered.

'I'd really feel much better about it,' he said with wholly insincere sincerity. 'I know you've said you don't need any money, but . . .'

'We-el, let's see now,' Ma said. 'What you think it's been worth to you, Doc?'

'Why—' he kept his smile warm, but there was a cold lump in his stomach. Several times already he had mentally totted up the money in the belts and divided it by two. 'Why, I wouldn't put a figure on it, Ma. It's worth whatever you say it is, and whatever you say is a hundred percent okay with me.'

'How'd five grand strike you?'

Five! He'd been expecting – well, he didn't know just what. But when people tapped you on a deal like this, it was usually for most of what you had. And there was nothing you could do but like it.

'It's not enough,' he declared, generous in his relief. 'I'd be getting a bargain at ten.'

'Knew you'd take it that way.' Ma wagged her head with satisfaction. 'Told Earl you would, didn't I, son? But it ain't for us, Doc. What I had in mind was, if you're sure that five or ten won't pinch you . . .'

'Ten. And it doesn't matter if it does pinch!'

'Well, I'd like you to pass it on to Pat Gangloni. I told you he was down there, I guess. He wasn't carryin' very heavy when he skipped, an' I been pretty concerned about him.'

'Good old Pat,' Doc said. 'I'll see that he gets it, Ma.'

'I'd o' helped him myself. But he was in an' out awful fast, an' I didn't have nothin' I could get at in a hurry. So,' she wrung his hand, 'I'm right pleased you'll be looking out for him. Know you mean to or you wouldn't say so.'

'It's as good as done,' Doc promised. 'After all, Pat's a mighty good friend of mine, too.'

They rode in the captain's car with Doc in the front seat between him and one of his crew, and Carol in the rear between the remaining two crewmen. Fog was thickening over San Diego, slowly descending upon the bay. The car crept through it cautiously, coming into the quay from the north, then circling the city's civic center, and returning from the south.

The boat was a sturdy fifty-footer, tied up about halfway down the long wharf. There were other seagoing craft on either side of it, a shrimp fisherman and a pleasure launch, but both were silent and dark. The captain parked the car and put the keys in the glove compartment. (It would be picked up by one of his many kinsmen.)

He opened the door, spoke quickly in Portuguese and English. 'Now, we are in a hurry; so we must be ready to go out with the tide. But we are not running. We go slow fast, yes?'

His teeth gleamed in a nervous smile. He got out and the others followed him, and they moved with unhurried haste across the quay. The captain leaped aboard, held out his hands to Carol. Doc landed on the deck a second behind her, and calling low-voiced instructions over his shoulder, the captain showed them to his tiny cabin. It was to be theirs for the voyage. He himself would bunk with the crew.

He closed the door behind him; and there was a murmuring of voices, a blurred confusion of sounds. Then the roar – quickly muted – of the boat's twin diesels. And they moved out into the bay.

The captain came back, drew the shades over the portholes and turned on the light. 'You will be very quiet, yes?' He smiled his white, nervous smile. 'On the water, the sound she travels far.'

He left again. Almost imperceptibly, the boat gathered speed. They slid deeper and deeper into the fog, and the gray mass of it closed in behind them.

Doc prowled about the cabin, automatically inspecting it as he did any place that was strange to him. He was looking for nothing in particular. Simply looking. Most top-drawer criminals have this habit. It had saved Doc's life several times, conversely bringing about the loss of another's life or other's lives on each occasion.

He checked the small shelf of books, and the first-aid cabinet. He looked under the bunk, smiling an apology at Carol who had lain down on it. He poked through the pigeonholes of the desk, located a key ring and unlocked and examined each of the drawers. Relocking them – and leaving their contents exactly as he had found them – he turned his attention to the heavy chest at the foot of the bunk.

It was padlocked at either end. Doc made a selection from the keys on the ring, found the appropriate ones on the first try and raised the heavy oak lid. There was a quantity of grayish blankets inside; also, bedded between them, several boxes of ammunition, two repeating rifles and two twelve-gauge double-barreled shotguns. Doc's eyes lit up. Then, almost absently, he loaded the shotguns, laid them at the top of the chest and lowered the lid. He put the locks back on their staples – not locked, although they appeared to be. That completed his inspection and its corollary activities, and he rehid the keys in the pigeonhole and fixed himself a drink.

Lying in the bunk, Carol watched her husband for a few moments, then turned on her side and closed her eyes. His behavior was merely another variation of a norm. If there was anything more than that behind it, he would tell her. When and if the telling became necessary.

She slept.

Almost immediately, it seemed, she came awake again.

Out there in the night, there was a peculiar echo to the boat's diesels. Or, no, it wasn't an echo, but the mounting purr of another engine. And against the blinded portholes, pushing stubbornly through the fog, was a fuzzy beam of light.

The cabin was dark. There was silence – tense, expectant – and then Doc's harsh whisper. Carol could see him now, feel him sitting at her side. And near the door she saw the white flash of the captain's teeth.

'You do what I tell you to, Pete. My wife and I will do the rest.'

'No! Please, senhor! I cannot – it is not necessary! Only a small launch, no more than three men, I know! All . . .'

'That makes it all the better.'

'Please! I tell you we do not have to! I swear it, and I know thees Coast Guard. Am I a stranger to them? Have I not made this same run many times? We will chat for a few moments, perhaps, and . . .'

'And they'll hold you up in the meantime. Find out who you are, and where you're headed. Get all the dope they need to have us nailed by a cruiser.'

'But – but—' there was a desperate sob in the darkness. 'But later, senhor? What of that? His position will have been known, and it will be known that I, my boat, was . . .'

'You can blame it on me. My wife and I slipped on board without your knowledge, and took charge of your guns and ammunition.'

'Ha! They will believe such a story?'

'Why not? It's a pretty good one.' Doc paused ominously. 'In fact, I'd say it was a lot better than the other one.'

'You say! It is easy for – what other one?'

'The one you'd have to tell Ma Santis. Not that it would do you any good, Pete. Nothing you could tell her would do any good.'

'But . . .'

The captain sighed heavily. The purr of the motor launch swelled to a sluggish drone.

'I don't like it either, Pete,' Doc said earnestly. 'I hate killing, and I particularly hate this. But what else can I do?'

'What else?' It scarcely sounded like the captain's voice. 'Yes, what else, senhor? What could possibly be dearer than one's own life?'

He turned and left. A moment later there was a cry of 'Ahoy, there! Ahoy, *Elena Isabella*!' Then a gentle bump and the scraping of wood against wood.

Doc cocked the shotguns. He handed one of them to Carol, and silently opened the two portholes.

There were three men in the launch: a gunner, the steersman, and its captain, a young lieutenant. He stood with one foot braced on the side of his boat, cap pushed back on his head. The steersman slouched nearby, an elbow hooked over the windshield. Hands in his pockets, the gunner stood by his stern-mounted machine gun.

Doc studied him. He put a restraining hand on Carol's arm. Wait! Perhaps the three would draw closer together.

'What's the big hurry, Pete?' The lieutenant spoke in an amiable drawl; a friend addressing a friend. 'Weren't trying to run away from me, were you?'

'R-run?' the captain laughed shakily. 'Who runs? Who is in a hurry?'

'Didn't bait up tonight, did you? Why not?'

'Why? Because I did so this afternoon. Also I iced, fueled, provisioned, keesed my wife . . .'

'Okay, okay,' the lieutenant chuckled. 'Got any coffee in the galley? Jack, bring us our bucket back there.'

The gunner came forward with a tin lunch pail. The lieutenant extended it upward, holding onto him for support.

'*Now!*' said Doc.

He got the two of them, almost cutting them in half at the waist with one double blast. They doubled over, toppled down into the dark water between the two boats. Carol's shot got the steersman in the face and chest. He was still alive when two of the fisherman's crew tossed him over the side, and blinded, faceless, he managed to struggle to the surface. Mercifully one of the men crushed his skull with an axe. Then they chopped a hole in the bottom of the launch, and leaped back aboard their own craft.

The diesels roared frantically. The boat lunged at the waves, lunged through them like a terrified thing. Running as though it could never run far enough, as though it would run forever. And then, as the hours passed, slowing. For what was done was done, and for now, at least, there was no need to run.

As for Carol and Doc . . .

They lay in one another's arms; replete, reunited at last. And Doc held her very close, stroked her head protectively. For she was his wife, much dearer to him than the average wife to the average husband. And if circumstances compelled him to think of her as an opponent – and he was not sure that they did, just yet – it was with no less love and a very great deal of regret.

She shivered against him, made muffled sounds against his chest. He emitted a few husbandly there-theres, murmured that everything was all right now. Then, realizing that she was laughing, he gave her a tender kiss. 'Now, what's so funny, hmmm?'

'Y-you! I – I – don't be angry, Doc, but . . .'

'Of course I won't be. Now what did I do that amused you?'

'N-nothing! It was – well, just you!' She snickered delightedly. 'You never really planned on staying in Mexico, did you? You never stopped hoping you could. Someday, somehow, you intended to do it. I could tell. I watched your expression when we were coming down on the train to San Diego, and – and . . .'

'And?'

'Well, you know. Now you can't. Not after that deal tonight.'

'Correction,' Doc said. 'Now *we* can't.'

CHAPTER FOURTEEN

The tiny area where El Rey is uncrowned king appears on no maps and, for very practical reasons, it has no official existence. This has led to the rumor that the place actually does not exist, that it is only an illusory haven conjured up into the minds of the wicked. And since no one with a good reputation for truth and veracity has ever returned from it . . .

Well, you see?

But it is there, all right.

Lying in a small coastal group of mountains, it suffers from sudden and drastic changes in climate. It is almost impossible to dress for it, the barely adequate clothes of one hour becoming a sweltering burden the next. And somehow, doubtless as an outgrowth of these climatic phenomena, one is always a little thirsty. Still, many tropical and semitropical climates have these same disadvantages, and worse. And there is this to be said for El Rey's kingdom: it is healthy. Disease is almost unknown. Even such man-created maladies as malnutrition and starvation are minus much of their normal potency, and a man may be almost consumed by them before he succumbs to them.

It is an excellent place in many ways. Healthy. Possessed of a climate to suit every taste. Protected by the largest per capita police force in the world. Yet there is constant grumbling among its expatriate guests. One of the commonest causes of complaint, strangely, is that all accommodations – everything one must buy – are strictly first class.

Not that they are exorbitantly priced, understand. On the contrary. A four-bathroom villa, which might cost several thousand a month in some French Riviera resort, will rent for no more than a few hundred. But you can get nothing for less than that. You must pay that few hundred. It is the same with food and drink, nothing but the very best; with clothes, cosmetics, tobacco, and a hundred other things. All quite reasonably priced for what they are, but still worrisomely expensive to people who have just so much money and can get no more.

El Rey manifests great concern over these complaints, but there is a sardonic twinkle in his ageless old eyes. Naturally, he provides only the best for his guests. Isn't it what they always wanted elsewhere? Didn't they insist on having it, regardless of cost? Well, then! He goes on to point out that less exquisite accommodations and material goods would encourage an undesirable type of immigrant; persons his present guests would not care to be identified with. For if they did, they obviously would not be what they were nor be where they were.

Watching their assets trickle, nay, pour away on every side, people scheme and struggle feverishly to economize. They cut down on food, they do without drink, they wear their clothes threadbare. And the result is that they are just as much out of pocket as if they had bought what they did without.

Which brings us to the subject of El Rey's bank, another cause for bitter complaint.

The bank makes no loans, of course. Who would it make them to? So the only available source of revenue is interest, paid by the depositor rather than to him. On balances of one hundred thousand dollars or more, the rate is six percent; but on lesser sums it rises simply, reaching a murderous twenty-five percent on amounts of fifty thousand and under. Briefly, it is almost imperative that a patron keep his account at or above the one hundred thousand figure. But he may not do this by a program of skimping and doing without. When one's monthly withdrawals fall under an arbitrary total – the approximate amount which it should cost him to live at the prevailing first-class scale – he becomes subject to certain 'inactive account' charges. And these, added to his withdrawals, invariably equal that total.

This is just about as it has to be, of course. El Rey must maintain an elaborately stocked commissary; and he can only do so on a fixed-patronage basis. Such is the rule in almost every first-class resort. A certain tariff is collected from every guest, and whether he uses what he pays for is strictly up to him.

To strike another analogy: no one is compeled to deposit his money in El Rey's bank. But the resort management, specifically the police, will assume no responsibility if it is stolen – as it is very likely to be. There is good reason to believe that the police themselves do the stealing from nondepositors. But there is no way of proving it, and certainly nothing to be done about it.

So the complaints go on. El Rey is unfair. You can't win against him. ('You would argue fairness with me, señor? But why should you expect to win?') He listens courteously to all grievances, but you get no satisfaction from him. He tosses your words back at you, answers questions with questions, retorts with biting and ironic parables. Tell him that such and such a thing is bad, and suggest a goodly substitute, and he will quote you the ancient proverb about the king with two sons named Either and Neither. 'An inquiry was made as to their character, señor. Were they good or bad boys, or which was the good and which the bad? And the king's reply? "Either is neither and Neither is either." '

People curse him. They call him the devil, and accuse him of thinking he is God. And El Rey will nod to either charge. 'But is there a difference, señor? Where the difference between punishment and reward when one gets only what he asks for?'

Most immigrants to the kingdom come in pairs, married couples or simply couples. For the journey is an arduous one, and it can seldom be made without the devoted assistance of another. In the beginning, each will handle his own money, carefully contributing an exact half of the common expenses. But this is awkward, it leads to arguments, and no matter how much the individual has he is never quite free of the specter of want. So very soon there is a casual discussion of the advantages of a joint account, and it is casually agreed that they should open one. And from then on – well, the outcome depends on which of the two is the shrewder, the more cold-blooded or requires the least sleep.

And whoever is the survivor, and thus has the account at his disposal, will not be alone long. He will be encouraged to seek out another partner, or one will seek him out. And when their association terminates, as it must, there will be still another.

The process goes on and on; inevitable, immutable. As simple as ABC.

Mention was made of El Rey's police; the protection they provide the populace. But this is a word of broad implications. If one is to protect, he may not annoy. He must remember that life belongs to the living. He will be wise to refrain from stepping over the line of his obvious duty to harry down a miscreant who may not exist.

Sluggings are unheard of in El Rey's dominion. No one is ever shot, stabbed, bludgeoned, strangled, or brought to death by the usual agencies of murder.

In fact, there are no murders. Officially, there are none. The very high death rate derives from the numerous suicides and the immigrant's proclivity for fatal accidents.

The fine swimming pools of the various villas are rarely used. The horses in the public stables grow fat for want of exercise, and the boats stand rotting in their docks. No one fishes, no one hunts, no one plays golf, tennis, or darts. Briefly, except for El Rey's annual grand ball, there is almost no social life. Anyone approaching another is suspect or suspicious.

Doc hardly knew what to do with himself. One day, a few months after his arrival, he took a walk up into the hills: and there, nestled in a pleasant valley and hidden from the city, he came upon a village. The one street was attractively cobblestoned; the buildings were freshly whitewashed. Drifting to him on the breeze came the smell of roasting peppery meat. The only people in sight were two men down near the end of the street, who were sweeping the cobblestones with long-handled brooms. Doc recognized them; he raised his hand in a half-salute. But not seeing him apparently, they finished their sweeping and disappeared inside a building.

'Yes, señor?' A blue-uniformed *carabinero* stepped out of a nearby doorway. 'I may be of service?'

'Nothing,' Doc smiled. 'I thought for a moment that I recognized those two men.'

'The streetsweepers? They are friends of yours?'

'Oh, no. Not at all. Hardly know them as a matter of fact.'

'I see. Well, they are newly arrived, those two. They will live here now, in case you should wonder about their absence from their usual haunts.'

Doc looked around: commented on the pleasing appearance of the place. The *carabinero* agreed that everything was indeed well kept. 'It is required. Each resident contributes such labor as he is able to.'

'Uh-huh,' Doc nodded. 'It's a cooperative, right? The labor is contributed in lieu of money.'

'That is right, señor.'

'Mmm-hmm.' Doc took another appreciative look around. 'Now, I was wondering. My wife and I have a very nice villa in the city, but . . .'

'No, señor. You would not be eligible for admittance here.'

'Well, now, I don't know about that,' Doc began. But the officer cut him off.

He *was* sure that Doc was not eligible. When he became so, he would be notified. 'You may depend on it, señor. Meanwhile, perhaps you would like to walk around – see what your future home will be like.'

Doc said that he would, and they started down the wide, sparkling street. Smoke rolled up from the chimneys of the houses, but not one stood in their doorways or looked out their windows, and hardly a sound came from any of them. The high dry air seemed unusually warm, and Doc paused and mopped his face. 'Where's the *cantina*? I'll buy the drinks.'

'There is none, señor. You can buy no drinks here.'

'Well, some coffee then.'

'That neither, señor. No drink or food of any kind.'

'No?' Doc frowned. 'You mean everything has to be brought out from the city? I don't think I'd like that.'

The officer slowly shook his head. 'You would not like it, señor. But, no, that is not what I mean. Nothing is brought from the city. Nothing but the people themselves.'

The words seemed to hang suspended in the air, a brooding message painted upon the silence. The *carabinero* seemed to study them, to look through them and on into Doc's eyes. And he spoke gently as though in answer to a question.

'Yes, señor, that is the how of it. No doubt you have already noticed the absence of a cemetery.'

'B-but—' Doc brushed a shaky hand across his mouth. 'B-but . . .'

That smell that filled the air. The odor of peppery, roasting flesh. Peppers could be had anywhere, for the picking, the asking, but the meat . . .

'Quite fitting, eh, señor? And such an easy transition. One need only live literally as he has always done figuratively.'

He smiled handsomely, and the gorge rose in Doc's throat; it was all he could do to keep from striking the man.

'Fitting?' he snarled. 'It – it's disgusting, that's what it is! It's hateful, hideous, inhuman . . .'

'Inhuman? But what has that to do with it, señor?'

'Don't get sarcastic with me! I've taken care of better men than you without . . .'

'I am sure of it. That is why you are here, yes? But wait—' he pointed. 'There is one who knows you, I believe.'

The man had just emerged from one of the houses. He was well over six feet tall, some five or six inches perhaps. And his normal weight should have been – indeed it *had* been – no less than two hundred and fifty pounds. But what it was now could not possibly be more than a third of that.

His eyes were enormous in the unfleshed skull's head of his face. His neck was no larger

210

than Doc's wrist. It was incredible that he could be alive; but of course, the climate is very healthy in El Rey's kingdom and many people live to a hundred years and more.

He staggered toward Doc, mouthing silently in his weakness. In his helpless silence, the exaggerated slowness of his movements, he was like a man caught up in some terrifying nightmare.

'Pat—' Doc's voice was a sickened whisper. 'Pat Gangloni.' Automatically, he recoiled from the apparition, and then, bracing himself he stepped forward deliberately and took Gangloni into his arms. 'It's all right, Pat. Take it easy, boy. You're okay now.' He patted the skeleton's shoulders, and Gangloni wept silently.

The *carabinero* watched them, an unaccustomed sympathy in his eyes.

'A sad case,' he murmured. 'Oh, but very sad. He is unable to resign himself. Already he has been here far longer than many.'

'Never mind that!' Doc turned on him angrily. 'Can you get me a car – a cab? Something to get him out of here?'

'We-el, yes. It will take a little time, but I can do it.'

'Well, do it then! Go on!'

'Your pardon, señor.' The *carabinero* didn't move. 'You would take him out of here, you said. Out of here to where?'

'Where? Why, to my home, naturally! Someplace where I can take care of him. Get him back on his feet.'

211

'And then, señor?'

'Then?'

'You will continue to provide for him?'

'Why, uh –' Doc slowed down a little. 'Well, yes, of course. I suppose so. I mean – uh . . .'

'You would be required to, señor. As long as you were able to provide for yourself. It would be so pointless otherwise. So cruel. Inhuman, as you said a moment ago.'

Gangloni began to shudder violently. He could not talk, but he could hear; like the man in the nightmare, he knew what was going on. Doc made a feeble attempt to free himself, and the skeleton arms tightened around him.

'He is a good friend, eh? You owe him much.' The *carabinero* was sympathy personified. 'I can understand. In this one, I would say, there is an inner fineness. He is a man of beliefs, principles – distorted and twisted perhaps, but . . .'

Doc abruptly broke free of Gangloni. He backed away on the cobblestones: grimacing, mumbling apologetically.

'I-I'll have to come back later. I – you know. Make some arrangements first. T-talk with my wife. Sure it'll be all right, b-but – but you know. How women are, I mean. I – I – Pat! *Don't look at me like that! Don't . . .*'

He turned and began to run.

On the suddenly chill breeze the carabinero's voice followed him.

'*Hasta la vista, señor.* Until we meet again.'

You tell yourself it is a bad dream. You tell yourself you have died – you, not the others – and have waked up in hell. But you know better. You know better. There is an end to dreams, and there is no end to this. And when people die they are dead – as who should know better than you?

El Rey does only what he has to. His criminal sanctuary is a big improvement over most. He does not kill you for your loot. He gives you value for your money. He runs a first-class place, and he could not do so if you were allowed to be miserly. Nor can he permit you to linger on when your money is gone. There would be no room for newcomers if he did; and allowed to accumulate, you and your kind would soon take over. You would be in his place, and he would be in yours up on that cobblestoned street with its sparkling whitewashed buildings. And he knows this. He and his native subjects know it. It explains their delight in irony, in symbolism; in constantly holding a mirror up to you so that you must see yourself as you are, and as they see you.

No, it is impossible to deceive yourself. The kingdom is there, maps and officialdom to the contrary. It is there, call it what you like. All things considered, it is probably the very best place of its kind. And its bad features, such as they are, derive not from El Rey but his guests.

He will not cheat you. He will not kill you. He cannot and will not provide for you, but he will not put an end to your life, no matter how long you live. And in that strangely salubrious climate, you seem to live an eternity.

In El Rey's dominion there is one night of the year – the night of the annual grand ball – when there are no 'suicides' or fatal 'accidents'. Everyone is politely but thoroughly searched before entering the *Palacio del Rey*, where the fete is held. Everyone is advised that any misfortune to a guest will be regarded with great displeasure. It has been many years since any such misfortune occurred, and the victim's plunge from a fourth-floor window actually was accidental. But everyone present was fined heavily, and the supposed instigator of the accident – the woman's husband – suffered total confiscation of his bank account. So today, not only does no one make an untoward move, but everyone shows the greatest concern for the welfare of everyone else. Raise your voice slightly, and you are immediately the target of a hundred anxious eyes. Reach suddenly for a handkerchief or cigarette, and a dozen people move toward you.

Very distinguished in white tie and tails, Doc McCoy stood on the promenade border of the great ballroom; beaming out over the swirling assemblage of dancers, bowing to this couple, smiling at that one, courteously inclining his head toward another. Perfectly groomed, his temples touched with gray, he was the very picture of a gentleman at ease, of well-bred charm. But he had seldom been less at ease, or more thoroughly miserable.

His physical discomfort – his numbed feet and aching back – was largely attributable to the wives of El Rey's two chief justices. Neither of the ladies was over five feet tall, yet their combined weight was considerably more than a quarter of a ton. And they were as near to being inexhaustible as anyone Doc had ever met. He had danced with them by turns, murmuring exquisite apologies as they walked giggling on his feet, whispering compliments as his back screamed at the constant bending. Oh, he had buttered up the ladies, but good; for they were known to be ogres in private, and virtually the masters of their henpecked husbands. Then, while he was silently congratulating himself, he had seen Carol dance by in the arms of the chief of police. And he knew that his agonized efforts had been wasted. The chief of police against the chief justices; if there was any advantage, it was on Carol's side. She might suffer for it, perhaps, if he became one of the dominion's suicides or accident victims. But that would do him no good whatsoever.

It was now more than an hour since he had seen either her or the chief of police, and his anxiety was growing. He would have to think very fast, or this might well be the last grand ball he would ever attend.

He made a final survey of the ballroom. Then

turning, apparently unseeing as a fat feminine hand waved to him across the throng; he strolled slowly down the palm-bordered promenade. And for some reason his mind went back to the long-ago day in Kansas; to the picnic grounds where he and Carol had gone after leaving the train.

'. . . *need to get acquainted again, Doc. We just about have to!*'

Doc smiled wryly to himself. Get acquainted? Oh no, they didn't need to. What had actually troubled them was that they knew each other too well. They lived by taking what they wanted. But getting rid of anyone who got in their way or ceased to be useful to them. It was a fixed pattern with them; it *was* them. And in the event of a showdown, they would show no more mercy toward each other than they had toward so many others. . .

Wrapped in thought, Doc sauntered down the promenade, absently glancing through the doorways of the innumerable parlors, drawing rooms and bars. From one of them, fat Ike Moss called a muffled greeting to him; gestured, his mouth stuffed to a long delicacy-laden table. But Doc smilingly shook his head, and passed on. Ike Moss, he thought distastefully. How gross, how completely lacking in a sense of propriety could the man be? Only last week his wife had drowned in her bath, yet here he was dressed to the nines, and gobbling down everything in sight.

Probably raided the icebox after he finished

her off, Doc thought. And he chuckled silently at the picture that came into his mind.

He came to a small billiard room; started on past it. Then he paused abruptly, straightened his shoulders, and went through the doorway.

Dr Max Vonderscheid was at the one pool table. His dwarfed hunchbacked body was dressed in rusty black, the tails of the ill-fitting suit almost touching the floor. And his gray leonine head rose only a few inches above the table. But still he appeared austerely handsome and dignified; and he sent the pool balls caroming about the green with almost magical accuracy.

He pocketed the last two with a difficult double-bank shot. Doc applauded lightly, and Vonderscheid set the cue on the floor butt down, and leaned on it looking at him. 'Yes, Herr McCoy? I may be of service to you?'

His speech was almost unaccented; Doc had observed that it almost always was except when he was around El Rey. He and El Rey were seemingly on very good terms, the latter making extraordinary concessions to the doctor with regard to rent and other expenses. Still, Vonderscheid had to have some kind of income, and he couldn't have much of a practice here.

'Yes?' There was a peculiar gleam in the hunchback's eyes. 'You cannot, perhaps, make up your mind?'

'Sorry,' Doc said hastily. 'I was so absorbed in watching your game that – but, yes, I believe

217

you can be of help to me. I, uh – the truth is I'm very worried about my wife. I don't think she's at all well.'

'I see. So?'

'Well –' Doc lowered his voice. 'It's of a highly confidential nature, Doctor. I'd want to discuss it in absolute privacy.'

Vonderscheid turned and glanced around the room, his gaze lingering for the merest moment on a palm-sheltered corner nook. Brows raised, he turned back to Doc again. 'This would seem to be private enough,' he said. 'Yes, this should do perfectly. So what is it about your wife, and why do you bring the matter to me?'

Doc began a cautious explanation. He had not nearly finished when Vonderscheid interrupted with an impatient gesture. 'If you please, Herr McCoy! So much talk for so commonplace a deed! You want me to examine your wife, yes? To suggest that she would do well to have one, with no mention that it is your suggestion. And then you wish me to tell her that she is in need of an operation. To convince her of it. And during the course of the operation, I am to . . .'

'No point in spelling it out,' Doc said quickly. 'After all, a great many people die in surgery. Now if you'd, uh, care to give me an estimate of your fee . . .'

'If I did it, there would be none. To remove either you or your wife from society would be both a pleasure and privilege. Unfortunately I

218

cannot do it. My name is Vonderscheid, not Katzenjammer. I am a doctor, not an assassin.'

'Now just a moment,' Doc frowned. 'I'm afraid you misunderstood me, Doctor. You surely don't think that I . . .'

'If you please!' Vonderscheid cut him off with a bang of the cue. 'Do not ask me what I think of you or your wife, of what you have done with your good bodies, your strong minds, your unlimited opportunities. If only half so much I had had, or poor Rudy Torrento . . .'

'So that's it,' Doc said, angrily sardonic. 'You and Rudy were friends, so naturally . . .'

He broke off. Vonderscheid had moved back a step, stood gripping the cue with both hands. He wagged it with an ominous movement, and Doc discovered he had nothing more to say.

'You are quite through, McCoy?' The doctor grinned at him furiously. 'Then I will finish. Rudy was my friend, yes. He was insane; he had been brutalized almost from birth; he had been made into what he was and he could not have been anything else. He had never had a friend, so I became one to him. I did not regard him as a criminal. No more, merely because I have broken laws, do I consider myself one. So! So that is all, Herr McCoy, except for two things. Your wife approached me only a few minutes ago with a proposition similar to your own. In fact, she should still be here,' he pointed to the cluster of potted palms. 'So in case you should wish to condole with one another . . .'

He laughed wickedly, tossed his billiard cue onto the table and walked out.

Doc bit his lip. He remained where he was for a moment, and then, with a kind of dreary nonchalance, he walked around the table and skirted the palms.

Carol had a portable bar drawn up in front of her. Silently he sat down at her side, and silently she fixed him a drink, her eyes warmly sympathetic. 'He was pretty rough on you, Doc. I'm sorry.'

'Oh, well,' Doc sighed. 'I hope he wasn't equally nasty with you, my dear.'

'I don't care about myself. I've been told off by experts. But someone like you, someone that everyone has always liked . . .'

She gave his hand a soothing pat, and Doc turned to her with thoughtful wonderment. 'Do you know,' he said, 'I believe you really love me.'

'Love you?' she frowned. 'Why, of course I do. Don't you love me?'

'Yes,' Doc nodded slowly. 'Yes, Carol, strangely enough I love you very much. I always have and I always will, and I could never love anyone else.'

'And I couldn't either. I – oh, Doc. *Doc!*'

'And it doesn't make any difference, does it, Carol? Or does it?'

'Does it?' She dabbed her eyes with her handkerchief. 'T-tell me it does, Doc, and I'll tell you it does. And what the hell difference will it make?'

Doc nodded vaguely. He refilled their glasses. In the palace tower a great bell began to toll the hour of twelve. And in the ballroom the band struck up the strains of *Home Sweet Home*.

'Well,' Carol said. 'I guess it's just about over, Doc.'

'Yes,' Doc said. 'Just about over, Carol.'

'You!' she said, and her voice was suddenly angry, frightened, tortured. 'I'll drink a toast to you, Doc darling!'

'Why, how kind of you,' Doc said, and he touched his glass to hers. 'What will it be?'

'To you! To you and our successful getaway!'

'And to you, my dear,' Doc said. 'And another such victory.'

THE END

WILD TOWN
by Jim Thompson

'My favourite crime novelist – often imitated but
never duplicated – is Jim Thompson'
Stephen King

When David 'Bugs' McKenna is hired as the
house detective for his hotel by Mike Hanlon,
the town's crippled millionaire, McKenna has
hopes that he can leave his violent past behind.
But the death of Dudley, the hotel auditor,
the disappearance of $5,000 and the unwanted
attentions of Lou Ford, the town's deputy sheriff,
and Joyce, Hanlon's beautiful, young wife,
mean that McKenna is looking at more trouble
than he can handle. And either a long, long
stretch in the State Pen or a longer stay in the
town cemetery . . .

'A blisteringly imaginative crime novelist . . .
mesmeric abilities as a story teller . . . he
outwrote James M. Cain at his most violent,
amoral, terse and fast-moving . . . a classic
American writer'
Kirkus Reviews

'Dashiell Hammett, Horace McCoy and Raymond
Chandler . . . none of these men ever wrote a
book within miles of Thompson's'
R.V. Cassil

0 552 13257 8

KING BLOOD
by Jim Thompson

Ike King was just about the biggest landowner in the Oklahoma territory. He'd built his empire with blood and violence and his sons planned to take it away using the same methods. First of all, Arlie murdered his brother Boz for the land but then Crich King came home. And he wanted his share. But Crich had a trail of corpses behind him and a United States Marshal hot on his heels. All of which made things mighty awkward for the blood-stained King family.

'If Raymond Chandler, Dashiell Hammett, and Cornell Woolrich could have joined together in some ungodly union and produced a literary offspring, Jim Thompson would be it'
Washington Post

'Read Jim Thompson and take a tour of hell'
The New Republic

0 552 13241 1

A SELECTED LIST OF CRIME NOVELS AVAILABLE FROM CORGI BOOKS

THE PRICES SHOWN BELOW WERE CORRECT AT THE TIME OF GOING TO PRESS. HOWEVER TRANSWORLD PUBLISHERS RESERVE THE RIGHT TO SHOW NEW RETAIL PRICES ON COVERS WHICH MAY DIFFER FROM THOSE PREVIOUSLY ADVERTISED IN THE TEXT OR ELSEWHERE.

☐	12792 2	THE COMPLETE STEEL	Catherine Aird	£2.50
☐	12793 0	HENRIETTA WHO?	Catherine Aird	£2.50
☐	12794 9	A LATE PHOENIX	Catherine Aird	£1.95
☐	13426 0	PARTING BREATH	Catherine Aird	£2.50
☐	13427 9	SLIGHT MOURNING	Catherine Aird	£2.50
☐	13237 3	BODIES	Robert Barnard	£2.50
☐	13368 X	CORPSE IN A GILDED CAGE	Robert Barnard	£2.50
☐	13129 6	THE DISPOSAL OF THE LIVING	Robert Barnard	£2.50
☐	13127 X	OUT OF THE BLACKOUT	Robert Barnard	£2.50
☐	13128 8	POLITICAL SUICIDE	Robert Barnard	£2.50
☐	13372 8	SHEER TORTURE	Robert Barnard	£2.50
☐	12804 X	WYCLIFFE AND THE PEA GREEN BOAT	W.J. Burley	£2.50
☐	12806 6	WYCLIFFE AND THE SCAPE GOAT	W.J. Burley	£2.50
☐	13232 2	WYCLIFFE AND THE BEALES	W.J. Burley	£2.50
☐	13231 4	WYCLIFFE AND THE FOUR JACKS	W.J. Burley	£2.50
☐	13433 3	WYCLIFFE IN PAUL'S COURT	W.J. Burley	£2.50
☐	13434 1	WYCLIFFE AND THE WILD GOOSE CHASE	W.J. Burley	£2.50
☐	10275 X	BELIEVE THIS, YOU'LL BELIEVE ANYTHING	James Hadley Chase	£1.95
☐	11251 8	CADE	James Hadley Chase	£1.95
☐	11096 5	THE DEAD STAY DUMB	James Hadley Chase	£1.95
☐	10715 8	I HOLD THE FOUR ACES	James Hadley Chase	£1.95
☐	11817 6	TRY THIS ONE FOR SIZE	James Hadley Chase	£1.95
☐	12275 0	WE'LL SHARE A DOUBLE FUNERAL	James Hadley Chase	£1.95
☐	11457 X	YOU HAVE YOURSELF A DEAL	James Hadley Chase	£1.95
☐	11308 5	YOU MUST BE KIDDING	James Hadley Chase	£1.95
☐	13235 7	MALICE DOMESTIC	Mollie Hardwick	£2.50
☐	13236 5	PARSON'S PLEASURE	Mollie Hardwick	£2.99
☐	13411 2	UNEASEFUL DEATH	Mollie Hardwick	£2.50
☐	13241 1	KING BLOOD	Jim Thompson	£2.99
☐	13257 8	WILD TOWN	Jim Thompson	£2.99

All Corgi/Bantam Books are available at your bookshop or newsagent, or can be ordered from the following address:

Corgi/Bantam Books,
Cash Sales Department, P.O. Box 11, Falmouth, Cornwall TR10 9EN

Please send a cheque or postal order (no currency) and allow 60p for postage and packing for the first book plus 25p for the second book and 15p for each additional book ordered up to a maximum charge of £1.90 in UK.

B.F.P.O. customers please allow 60p for the first book, 25p for the second book plus 15p per copy for the next 7 books, thereafter 9p per book.

Overseas customers, including Eire, please allow £1.25 for postage and packing for the first book, 75p for the second book, and 28p for each subsequent title ordered.